Praise for *light of your body*

"These stories travel the infinite borders of life-death-rebirth, in the lush storytelling language of *poesía*. The language of *abuelitas, abuelitos*, the Ancestors, the light of our bodies. The Serpent Goddess Coatlicue whispers, 'I am the mother of myself ... And this is how the world never ends.' A prayer. A blessing."

—Alma Luz Villanueva, author of *Song of the Golden Scorpio*

In *the light of your body*, ire'ne lara silva demonstrates mastery of prosody, rhythm, incantation, and storytelling. Like Cormac McCarthy—and with as much syntactical *duende*—she can lead us in and out of worlds, allow us to pass between many borders, between the dead and the living, the real and the imagined, between pre-Covid consciousness and now. [...] These rhythms, images and stories are a passport to cross into the spirit world, like a coyote leading across a border, or Charon on the River Styx, and they can bring the reader into that liminal space, that border in between, in and out of Nepantla.

—Daniel Chacón, author of *The Last Philosopher in Texas: Fiction and Superstitions*

"Like a stealth panther gliding toward you, ire'ne lara silva's magical stories will stop you in your tracks to ponder the sublime peril crouching closer. You'll find you can't resist the power, the mystery of stories so intimate that you feel yourself inside mystical creatures that transform you. Whether the alchemist of blue horses or nesting hummingbirds or the musicians named Los Ocoletes wandering in another realm or the enigmatic woman with a penchant for hibiscus tacos, silva brings to life characters so otherworldly that you want to inhabit the spaces that see, feel, smell and love from such distinct perspectives."

— Emma Pérez, author of *Testimony of Shifter* and *Gulf Dreams*

"These stories are meant to sit with you, plumb into the depths of your body as they explore what is ephemeral & what is eternal about our existence on this earth. Written at times with humor, with fierceness, with whimsy, with tenderness & always with love, *the light of your body* shines light on souls that endure beauty, pain, longing, love, loss and bliss, artfully reaffirming that every one of us is a miracle—just for being."

—Natalia Sylvester, author of *Running* and *Breathe and Count Back from Ten*

"*the light of your body* is a feast of passion and lush delights. silva traverses the landscape of Chicano identity in this collection of fearsome and earthy loves .... Gorgeous and haunting, these stories traverse borders of time and space, of the body, of the soul, and lay open the intricacies of the heart.

—Marcela Fuentes, author of *Malas*

the light of your body

ire'ne lara silva

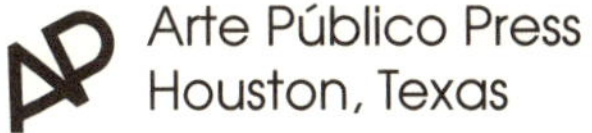
Arte Público Press
Houston, Texas

the light of your body is published in part with support from the Alice Kleberg Reynolds Foundation. We are grateful for their support.

"hibiscus tacos" was first published as a limited edition bilingual chapbook by Alabrava Press.

Recovering the past, creating the future

Arte Público Press
University of Houston
4902 Gulf Fwy, Bldg 19, Rm 100
Houston, Texas 77204-2004

Cover design by Ryan Hoston
Cover art by Moisés S. L. Lara

♾ The paper used in this publication meets the requirements of the American National Standard for Information Sciences—Permanence of Paper for Printed Library Materials, ANSI Z39.48-1984.

Printed in the United States of America

26 27 28 4 3 2 1

Acknowledgments

With thanks to the following publications in which earlier versions of these stories appeared:

"border as womb emptied of night and swallows" in *Nepantla Familias: A Mexican-American Anthology of Literature on Families in Between Worlds,* edited by Sergio Troncoso
"hibiscus tacos" in *The Rumpus*
"huitzitzilin" in *Blue Mesa Review*
"in this dream of blue horses" in *Windward Review*
"the light of your body" and "xoxōtlameh, my love" in *Yellow Medicine Review*
"los ocelotes del norte" in *Acentos Review*
"marzipan" in *The Thing Itself*
"of the green grasses" in *Pleiades Review*
"of the seedling wife" in *Apogee Journal*
"serpents-her-skirt" in *The Journal of Latina Critical Feminism*
"song of the burning woman" in *Alaska Quarterly Review*
"with wings, hooves, and horns" in *World Literature Today*

Additionally:

"border as womb emptied of night and swallows" is a line of poetry by Rodney Gómez

"in this dream of blue horses" was inspired by the following article: https://www.livescience.com/9589-surprising-history-america-wild-horses.html

"los ocelotes del norte" was inspired by Los Tigres del Norte and the art of Isaac Cordal

"prophecy" was inspired in part by the painting by Octavio Quintanilla, *hoy pensé en ti*

for my brother, Moisés, who on his deathbed,
asked me to read him my stories

contents

Con toda palabra
Con toda sonrisa
Con toda mirada
Con toda caricia
Me acerco al agua
Bebiendo tu beso
La luz de tu cara
La luz de tu cuerpo

—Lhasa de Sela, “Con toda palabra”

tlaquetzqui

Every time I start a new story, it's like I have to remember how to tell a story all over again. Like my body's forgotten how to move so it can dance, like my lungs have forgotten how to breathe so I can sing the long notes, like words are impossible things that spin and spin without going in the direction I want them to go.

This feeling reminds me of a road trip I took. The altitude increasing with every mile. People told me to stay hydrated, that I might get fatigued, that it might cause headaches. No one told me my mucus would become bloody. That it'd be a full-time job to soothe my chapped lips. Or that the increasingly clear night skies would drive away all sleep. I wanted to see the stars more than I wanted anything.

That's why I don't give up on telling new stories. Even if my nose is bloody. Even if I can't sleep. Stories bring the stars closer.

I have a story to tell you. Or rather, I have a story to tell you about telling a story. But I'm taking my time getting started because I might not know you as well as I think I do. I might not know you at all. You might surprise me with a bark of laughter or tears when that wasn't what I meant to provoke in you. When you hear or read this story, I might not have the chance to remind you who I am or what kind of stories I tell.

I tell people all the time that I believe stories are medicine. Better said, some stories are medicine. Other stories are trash. And some stories are poison. It's the nature of some medicine that too much of it can be poison. But what is living if not the constant work of titration? What's too much? What's not enough?

My mother told me a long time ago, "If a ghost comes to you, then that ghost is yours."

I beg to differ. There are a lot of ghosts. You shouldn't listen to all of them. You shouldn't always do what they want. Or even let them stay around. This is the world of the living. Don't ever forget that. Stake your claim. Say, "These are my walls. This is my home. This is my life. This is who I love. These are my choices. And it's time for you to go."

Of course, it's different if you go around invoking them and asking them for help. Asking them for protection. Saying and saying their names. Personally, I think Selena and Gloria in the afterlife are like, "Sheesh, don't y'all have some ancestors or some saints to call on? Like, I didn't sign up for all these invocations making me run around all creation for you people."

It's also different if you're just plain haunted. If you live in a house or on ground with stubborn spirits or the mess they left behind. I've known people with ghosts that followed them from place to place. Known people who did things they shouldn't have and those ghosts never let them live in peace. Known people with haunted blood, their fathers or mothers having passed down all their ghosts. And not the peaceful, wisdom-offering kind of ghosts either.

People are like, "The ancestors this" and "the ancestors that." But apparently they forgot about our history because a lot of our ancestors died furious, died stark raving mad, died tortured, died despairing. Death doesn't heal everything, doesn't put everything magically back together and make it whole. So, you gotta be careful about what you call on.

I know it's disappointing to think this. But the same way there are stupid people, there are stupid ancestors. You know as well as I do that age doesn't necessarily mean wisdom. There are a lot of people that never dedicated themselves to becoming elders, the kind you could depend on and learn from. And a lot of the people that did do that, well, when they died, they erased themselves from our plane of existence and were able to peacefully rejoin the creative energy of the universe or Nature or the Great Spirit or whatever they thought heaven was.

My mother would always say death wasn't to be feared. Because when you died, you didn't have to worry anymore, didn't have to work anymore, didn't have to be sick anymore. Didn't have to feel the tiredness in your bones anymore. So, in some ways, I can be grateful that she went pretty young. Because I know she wasn't happy. She fought like hell, but how much fight can you have in you when life holds a lot of suffering?

I'm almost as old as my mother was when she passed. And apparently, it's taken me this long to realize that not being afraid of death is easy when you're poor and struggling and in pain and worried out of your mind. It's completely something else when life is sweet. And my life is sweet.

I wake up most mornings looking out a big window with all of the sky in it. Some mornings, his arms are around me, his scent all around me. And depending on how my bladder's feeling, I either wriggle out of his arms or snuggle in closer. When

Cruz isn't there, I stretch my whole body this way and that and bury my face in the pillow until I need to breathe.

It's different. This kind of loving when you're older. Still heady. That feeling like hunger to have them near, to hear their voice, to look at them, to touch them and be touched by them.

What's different though is that after a while, you want them to go away. They don't need to be there all the time. Even when I was young, I thought Diego and Frida's separate houses were a great idea. Everybody worries about their own breakfast, lunch and dinner. Keep your things where you like them. Take care of your own laundry. Not having to tell anyone when or why you're coming and going. Living alone is a daily paradise. Sleep when you want. Eat when you want. Do what you want. Read or take a shower or sing like a banshee or workout or give yourself half a dozen orgasms in a row. Whatever you want.

My home is like my Fortress of Solitude. It's like my burrow, my cave, my castle, my own turtle shell. Where I'm safest and strongest. You can't let just anyone into your home or your bed or your body. People leave things behind. Their emotions, their fragmented ghosts, their hungers. But every now and then, you come across somebody who feels like your other self. And it's interesting, because since neither of you are young anymore, there are stories and stories and stories to tell each other.

Really, that's what I think everything is made of. The sunlight is a story the sun tells. The night is a story the stars tell. Trees and flowers and grass are stories the earth tells. Every man, woman, child, beast, bird and fish is a story life tells. Our bodies are stories time tells. Desire is a story skin tells skin, mouth tells mouth, heat tells heat. Love is trusting someone with your stories and holding someone else's stories. Healing is a story we tell our bodies and a story our bodies tell back to us.

My mother was big on meditation. I'm not sure that she was ever not meditating. Meditating while she was gardening. Meditating while she was cooking. Meditating when she was driving. She'd say, "You just have to concentrate. Make your mind blank. Like looking at clouds."

I've never been able to do it. I'm either thinking or talking or dreaming or doing. Otherwise, I'm asleep. I could never be one of those Buddhist monks in the Tibetan mountains, chanting for peace all their lives. I could maybe do it if I spent all my days scrubbing floors or pulling weeds, but I hate doing both those things, so that's out. The only kind of meditation I ever truly got was the one where you breathe in all the hurt, pain and destruction in the world and breathe out peace and compassion. Of course, I'm not sure that I was supposed to be visualizing a dragon in my chest that ate all the darkness and roared out fire. Most people would say fire wasn't a good representation of peace and compassion, but apparently, that's what my peace and compassion look like.

Made me think of that Aztec goddess known as the eater of filth. They call her the goddess of sex, filth and prostitutes, but she was also the one who purified sinners and brought them to redemption. But I'm no Marvin Gaye to be running around doing some sexual healing, and I find forgiveness kind of difficult.

So that's probably why I ended up deciding stories were my way of making medicine. People have some crazy ideas about what medicine in the form of stories is. I'm not making chicken soup here. This isn't candy sweet cherry cough drops or your favorite fluffy blanket. I'm not talking about the soft daily medicine—what you can eat or drink every day or laughter or singing or the sunshine or the wind your body and spirit need. I'm talking about the fierce medicine—what it takes to take hold of the illness in the body or in the world and force it out. I'm talking about taking it into your hands and making it surrender to your will. I'm talking about taking that pain and hurt and pushing it into a blazing fire and holding it in the fire with your bare hands and then bringing it out as something new, something renewed.

And so sometimes, ghosts and things find you when they realize you're ferocious enough to listen to their stories. To eat the filth and swallow it. To cast it into the burning cauldron of your belly. Ferocious enough to feed the fire and feed the fire and make your soul into an immense bellows that just builds the fire up higher and higher.

One time my mother said, "The dead eat a lot less than the living." But then she didn't say anything else. Years after she died, when I was visiting my father, I noticed that the door next to the kitchen would open by itself at all hours of the day and night. If my father was there to witness it, he would just call out, "*¡Entre,* Socorro!"

I must have looked at him funny 'cause all he said was, "That's what you do when doors open by themselves."

That night, I placed a small glass of water, a couple flowers, a small mound of beans and a small pile of *masa harina* on the shelf above the door. The door never opened again while I was there.

We make a big fuss about the Day of the Dead and all the food and providing all the favorites of the dead. My mother remembered the tables laden with food at the cemeteries in South Texas, and how the living wouldn't touch the food until the night had passed. What most people don't realize is that what's important is the care with which the food is made, the thought that goes into choosing it, making the trip to take the food or build the altar, the ways in which the food and the flowers and the photos help us to focus our attention and our emotions. I figure that's what my mother meant. That what we feed our departed loved ones is our attention, our love, our memory. The food is only a vessel. As our bodies are only vessels.

It's relatively easy to hear ghosts. The same way you can hear the living. And like the living, you can shut out whatever voices you want. It's all about concentration. We know animals speak and signal to each other, but it took me years to realize the trees were speaking. More years to distinguish the different dialects of mesquites and *huizaches*, *retamas* and pecans, oaks and cottonwoods, anacuas and cedars, *azebuches* and tallows. The wind moves through each kind of tree differently, and even when the leaves are still, the branches and the trunks and the roots are all humming. Sometimes to hear the roots, I lay down on the ground, arms outspread, face cheek to cheek with the earth.

The young trees just seem to chatter about the joy of growing and stretching their limbs, celebrate dew and rain, marvel at their changing leaves every spring and summer and fall. The fruit trees spend the days and nights singing their flowers into being and then cradling their growing bundles of sweetness. You'd think they'd weep in the fall and winter when their leaves fall, but no, they're full of gleeful shrieking as their branches lighten and they feel the sun on their bark. I've walked among all kinds of trees … in orchards, in forests, in *monte* thick with thorned branches.

When I was much younger, I liked to walk alongside creeks and rivers, ponds and lakes. It seemed like I'd almost always find an old, wide tree with thick roots exposed. I liked to lay down between them, then watch the ripples in the water or the clouds in the sky or the dappled sunshine through the leaves. Didn't matter if it was twenty degrees or a hundred. How I loved feeling like the earth was cradling me.

I didn't grow up around oak trees. That's probably why it took me longer to understand them. Their voices are at a lower register. And the older they are, the slower they speak. As if time was moving at a different pace for them. Or maybe I was the one that needed to be older. To realize that they weren't just grumbling. To be patient enough to stop and listen. I needed all those years to be able to carry their stories.

When I was younger, I didn't want to hurt. I spent my youth running away from pain and the memory of pain. There were years when I would have willingly changed my name and forgotten who I was to free myself from the stories I carried. I ran as far and as fast as I could. It took me decades to stop running, and then life served me pain and beauty in equal measures and taught me medicine.

I don't claim to know anything more than the bare beginning of what medicine is. But I'm listening now.

I was listening when I started to understand what the oak trees were saying. It started as a shushing like static broken with a few clear words: "I eat shush shush the ash shush shush and eat shush shush the ash." There was keening, high and wild, and moaning, low and ruined. I didn't sob though I wanted to, the pressure in my chest building and building. My left eye was streaming tears, my right eye clear and dry. Since I was a child that was the sign that I was crying someone else's tears, not my own.

I had a vision when I was twenty-seven. In the vision, I was walking through a desert and the sun was beating down on my head and I could barely see in front of me. I was carrying an immense *olla* on my back. There were straps around my forehead, around my shoulders, around my hips, in my hands. Every part of my body felt like it was burning, every muscle like it was about to burst. It felt like I'd been carrying the *olla* all my life, like the rough clay of it had been grafted onto my skin. I could feel the liquid in it moving with every step, and I understood what I was carrying. The *olla* was filled to the brim with tears. Not my tears but my ancestors'. The sun was burning the top of my head and each step was harder to take than the one before. Until I could barely breathe from the pain of carrying those tears. My steps slowed. My feet were barely moving. Until I couldn't move anymore. I bent my knees until the base of the *olla* was resting on the ground. I loosened the straps. A cloud covered the sun. I breathed. And I thought about walking away. About leaving the *olla* in the desert. Letting the heat of the sun dry it until it held nothing but salt. Thought about how much easier it would be to walk to wherever I was going without the weight of the *olla,* without the weight of all those tears that weren't mine.

I'm not sure what made me fasten all the straps around my body again. Why I took a deep breath and pulled up the weight with my weary back and my weary hands. Why I let the weight settle on me again, fitting against me as if the *olla* had been made to be carried by me and only me. Maybe that's why I did it. Because they were mine and only I could carry them. And in the vision, I walked on, knowing the only way to make the *olla* lighter was to cry all the tears it carried with my own eyes.

That's what I felt when I started listening to the oak trees. Not all of them. But a lot of them. Old ones. Young ones. The saplings reminded of the way babies fell asleep after long fits of crying, their little bodies twitching, their limbs restless, their breath still catching in half sobs.

"*Gemir y gemir*," I seemed to remember my mother saying. She would pat babies to sleep without singing them lullabies. Just a monotonous *hmm hmm hmm mmh* that would repeat over and over again. It was the only way I knew to put babies to sleep and it never failed. So when I first heard the saplings with their half-sobs, I placed the palms of my hands on their slender trucks and patted them without words, only long interlocking chains of *hmm hmm hmm mmh*. Until I could feel their breaths even out and their leaves moving peacefully.

I never told my mother and she never asked, but at twenty-four I decided I wouldn't have children. For many different reasons, but the one that was clearest to me was that I didn't want to pass down the depression, the addiction, the violence, the abuse or the shadows I had inherited. I said there would be no children of my body. And there weren't. Children of my heart is a different thing. But that is a different story.

The oak trees couldn't make my choice. Couldn't decide to forsake the making of acorns. Their only choice was to make seeds or die. To live was to make seeds and risk what and how much they'd inherit. And they, like many of us, found reasons to keep on going. For the blue sky. For the rain. For the setting of the sun. For the stars. For the wind. For the hours which only grew sweeter as they accumulated. But don't think they didn't weep. Don't think they didn't pass on their memories and their shadows and their hurts down through their seeds.

"I eat the ash and eat the ash," I heard, "I eat the ash and eat the ash." And it mixed with the other voices, "I carry the bones of my dead … where are the bones of my dead … their blood lingers … I hold their last breaths …"

I don't have enough hands to pat all the trees. I don't have enough air in my lungs for a million *hmm hmm hmm mmhs*. I don't have enough eyes to cry for them. I am still carrying the *olla* of my ancestors' tears. It's been more than twenty-five years since my vision, and the *olla* still chafes along the grooves worn deep, deep into me. I've become stronger. I haven't had to put the *olla* down in twenty-five years. But that doesn't mean it isn't heavy. My heart cries as many tears as it can before it has to stop. Always knowing there are more waiting.

I spend as much time as I can with the trees. It isn't always a matter of hours. Isn't always a matter of how many tears I can shed. Sometimes it has to do with how much I can stand to listen to, how many of their stories I can hold. The first time I touched one of the oldest trees, I fell to my knees and lost my own name.

Cruz found me twelve hours later, shivering and mute. He took me to my home. Made me coffee and pressed the mug into my hands. Took off my muddied clothes and pushed me into the shower. Washed my hair and my face, warmed me with his hands and the soap and the hot, hot water. He wrapped me in towels and brushed my hair slowly while I leaned against him. He made me oatmeal, thick and milky, sweet with *piloncillo*, sharp with cinnamon. I started crying again when he led me to my bed and wrapped himself around me. I fell asleep like those weary babies, hiccupping and twitching, breathing in the scent of his neck as if I would lose my way without it.

Days passed and I was like a wounded creature, wandering from room to room, laying in the dark. I ate sometimes. I tried not to think. I cried when I remembered and when I didn't. Cried when I was alone and when Cruz was there. My skin, my flesh, my bones hurt with the story the oak tree had given me.

From when I was very young, I had a talent for *sobadas*. *Sobar* is not the same as "to massage." Massage has to do with training and technique, with muscles and tendons and ligaments. To *sobar* is to read a body, its energies and its pains, its memories and its resistances. My hands are always warm but when I was starting a *sobada*, they would heat up as if there were burning charcoals in my palms. Sometimes I would close my eyes to better be able to follow the lines I could see arcing from one place to another. I would sweat, no matter how cold the room was. It felt as if I was pulling the healing force down from the sky and it was pulsing through me and into the person. Sometimes I'd find myself pulling their limbs or twisting their entire bodies, trying to wring out of them what needed to be wrung out. Finally, I'd release them, after sweeping over them with my hands, dusting the remainders of pain and shadows off them. Back then, I wouldn't be tired afterwards. I'd feel a spiraling elation while I washed my hands with salt and then went outside to breathe fresh air while the sun or the moon shown down on me.

And then there were two decades where I couldn't do *sobadas* or *limpias* anymore. I still knew what to do. I could still read energies and bodies. But something had changed, and I didn't know how to fix it. Before, the healing would come through me and into the person, pushing the pain out. Without knowing how or why it had happened, all of that reversed direction. There was no healing coming through me. Instead, I was eating all of their pain. They'd feel better after a *sobada* or a *limpia,* but I'd spend entire days racked with pain, barely able to move or sleep. So, I learned not to reach out, not to offer, not to touch, when I saw a person in pain. In those years, I couldn't afford to incapacitate myself in any way. And I didn't have the energy or time or heart to figure out what had changed. What had gone wrong. If I had done or was doing something wrong.

My life changed five years ago. And slowly, I started making my way back to being a *sobadora*. I'm still much more cautious about who and when than I was when I was young. I'm not paralyzed with pain anymore. Sometimes I think it was something I was supposed to learn. What it was to be able to heal and then not to be able. What it was to learn to choose carefully where to give my energy. What it was for other things in life to need so much of me, there was very little to spare. What it was to learn taking in the pain of others and having to move it through myself—through my *entrañas* and my heart. The small, theoretical dragon breathing fire in my chest wasn't enough anymore. I needed a beast of a dragon, so large I could barely envision all of it, one that overran the limits of my body and my imagination. Fire isn't for everyone, but it's always been the most beautiful thing I know.

And so, while the oak tree's story had caused me to collapse, I knew what to do afterwards. Knew to let myself be taken care of. Knew to let myself shed all the tears I could shed. Knew to sleep all the hours I could sleep. Knew the hours I spent staring at the sky through my bedroom window were not wasted. Not while I fed the dragon and let it roar fire and more fire inside of me.

Medicine is often bitter. The knowledge of healing is often painful. To know all the ways the body can be broken, all the ways the body breaks itself when the heart is broken, all the ways the body curls in around itself, twists itself, deforms itself trying to live with its pain. Anyone who says healing is all joy and light has no idea what they are talking about. Or they are predators feeding on the vulnerable.

I don't know what my mother thought of history in the abstract. I know she carried stories the way few people seem to carry them, especially "educated" people. I never knew her mother, except through her stories. I learned to cook through stories, not recipes. I learned highways and directions and weather through stories, not maps or news reports. She'd often start with one story, which would link to another story and then another story. I say stories because they weren't memories the way most people share their memories. They were stories. With beginnings and endings and things to learn. Sad stories and beautiful stories and funny stories and stories that couldn't be described. Sometimes, just because, she'd start relating long chains of things she knew, like the birth dates of dozens of relatives, living and dead, like the names of flowers she'd grown in one house and another, last year and a decade before and when she was a child.

Sometimes, and especially when you start learning the history of your people as an adult, all you can feel is rage. There is nowhere to put all of it. No way to contain all of it. You want to weep for the rest of your life. You want to burn things down. You want to know why you were never told. Why other people didn't know. How things could have happened that way. How things can be the way they are now. Why people seem to be asleep. And there are so many directions to take. To dismiss it all as the past. To let it make you bitter. To let it make you give up. To turn into a fiery activist. To become an artist. To become a teacher. To become a criminal. To let it turn you to things I can't even stomach enough to articulate.

I knew the oak tree's story. I had read about it. Read about many of those stories. Knew it had happened, many times in many places. Knew that for as many stories as were told, there were many, many more that weren't recorded. Black bodies and brown bodies hung from trees, tortured, hanged, shot, killed. For decades, for centuries, before and after recorded accounts.

What I hadn't known was that the trees remembered. That their blood and their screams had sunken into their roots, run through their veins, been passed on to thousands and thousands of their seeds. That all the trees wept together. That the passing of the years hadn't dulled their memories. The same way that earth soaked in our blood forgot nothing.

I had known the oak tree's story. I had carried it myself as a story of my people. But I hadn't carried it the way the oak tree did, with blood and memory, with curses and prayers exhaled in dying breaths.

So, I fed the dragon and repeated what I'd heard the oak trees say: "I eat the ash and I eat the ash. I eat the ash and I eat the ash." I fed the dragon, and the fire roared and I ate the ash. And from the ash, I made medicine. I can't tell you how I made the medicine—not because there are no words, but because there are some things you must learn by doing. How I made my medicine is mine to know.

Some people believe healing is meant to restore the body to what it was before. As if no scar should remain, as if no memory should remain, as if everything could return to what it was before. That is not healing. Forgetting is not medicine. You learn nothing from forgetting—not how to avoid future wounds, not compassion, not understanding, not the weight of things. Forgetting doesn't teach you how to listen. Doesn't teach you how to carry stories.

So I slept and I cried and I let Cruz hold me. I fed the dragon, and it roared and I ate the ash and I made medicine. And then I went out into the woods. I sat by the oldest oak tree, almost impossible to follow the full reach of its thick branches. I sat and reached out to it with my hot palms. I listened. I listened. I offered my medicine. It offered me its medicine. And then it sent me out, to pat all of its tender offspring with my hands, humming and humming.

border as womb emptied of night and swallows

I followed you here. I'd follow you anywhere. My father said it wasn't right. That we had it backwards. That it was the woman who was supposed to follow her husband. But that never mattered to me. I'd never do anything that would keep us apart. What I am is yours. I am yours even when you are away. When I am alone. I am yours for as long as I breathe and even after. I am yours for as long as you want me.

Memory brought you here. Brought us here. Your history is here. Your family. Your parents and grandparents and great-grandparents. Your siblings and nieces and nephews. When we were in Ithaca, all you could talk about was how much you missed them. How much you missed this land and the endless horizons and the wind and the heat and the sunsets and the rose-colored fog in the morning and the sugar cane burning and the river and driving to South Padre Island and the roasted corn and the shaved ice with syrup and El Pato's and the *botanas* and the *chorizo* from San Manuel and the *taquitos de trompo* served with *frijoles a la charra* and baked potatoes and the *cabrito al carbón* on the other side of the border. You missed everything, even the scent of the air and the heat of the nights and the feel of the earth. To you, the Rio Grande Valley wasn't simply a place on a map—the name itself was an incantation. Earth and sun and magic all at once.

I promised you I'd follow you. To love you is to live here. The palm trees lining the highways and the fruit-bearing trees in the orange groves and the mesquites everywhere all whisper your name to me.

Most nights, when you're at work, I go for long drives. On the freeways where all the lights blur, the access roads when I want to see things pass by more slowly. Interstates, state roads, county roads, farm to market roads, connecting one town to the next. Some towns hardly more than a city limit sign, two houses and a gas station. Some nights I turn onto caliche roads, counting the lights of trailer parks, surprised suddenly by what look like little houses with parking lots and too many cars. Some of them bars without permits, most of them brothels. I sit at truck stop diners, drinking cup after cup of coffee. I have something sweet. Pancakes. Or pie. Or cake. Then more coffee until I can bear to go back out again and devour the miles. Windows open and the road screaming past. Everywhere I see roadside *descansos*, wooden crosses piled with plastic flowers and ribbons and beads. All the tattered and bright colors of someone's grief.

Some nights I listen to the radio, and then I'm almost happy. I shout-sing along. Doesn't matter what it is—top forty, country music, the songs I remember from the nineties, The Cure, The Cranberries, new and old Tejano, Michael Salgado and Intocable, and old *conjuntos*, Los Relámpagos and Los Tigres del Norte and Los Cadetes de Linares looping over and over again.

When the whispers began, I tried to outrun them, first on the treadmill then at the university track. I tried weights. I tried punching the bag in the garage. I tried jerking off. I tried drinking. At home and then at the bar down the street. And then at the icehouse on the far edge of town. I thought about going across the border to the bars in Reynosa or Progreso, thought about how it wasn't safe anymore, thought about how, even on good days, it pissed me off to deal with the border patrol and the checkpoints. I didn't grow up like you—I wasn't used to their omnipresence, to the constant questioning of my citizenship. I thought I might take a swing at one of them if I was drunk. So I stayed away from the bridges that would take me across. I stayed on the roads. Listened to the wind and the music.

I'm always home by the time the sun rises. Early enough to shed all my clothes and warm our bed and for my eyes to become bleary with sleep before you arrive. I hear your car park in the driveway, hear your keys at the door, hear you make tea and drink it in the kitchen, hear the groan when you take off your shoes. And you sit there for a bit and breathe. And when you come to bed, I greet you with open arms and hold you tight. You tuck your face into my neck and I breathe in the scent of your hair. And you tell me about your day. Sometimes we laugh. Sometimes we cry. And we lie there, breathing together until the alarm goes off, and I have to leave you, get showered and dressed, go to work. I sleep enough, I guess. I stay awake all day. I sleep on the nights you're home with me. The rest of the time, it's an hour here, an hour there. I start awake, find myself patting my own chest, feel a phantom warmth smaller than the palm of my hand over my heart.

Unlike you, no one's life depends on how awake I am. I don't love my job. But it's a living and sometimes that's enough. I took it when we moved here and you were starting your residency. I sit in a cubicle all day, looking over reports, checking numbers and names, comparing endless streams of data for eight hours. The phone never stops ringing with people calling to ask me questions. For lunch, I walk over to the *taquería* next door. Sit in the corner by the jukebox, back to the door, and eat my enchiladas while I take in the music. The waitress brings me *limonada* without having to ask me. There's a streak of grey in her hair. She calls me, *m'ijo,* asks after you, and always tells me to get some rest, that I'm too young to have such tired-looking eyes. I pat the hand she puts on my shoulder and tell her in Spanish that I know that my mother, from the other world, would thank her for taking such good care of me. The name tag on her ruffled Mexican blouse says, Altagracia. You've never met her, but she knows all about you—how we met, your family, your job, your favorite foods, what we've done every weekend and every holiday for the last five years. She adds the '*ita*' of affection to your name, calls you, "*la Raquelita*," and I don't doubt that she'd greet you like a long-lost daughter if you ever walked in through the door.

On the way back to my little beige cubicle, the *urracas* make their harsh cries, wings moving this way and that, dark eyes following my steps. I think of you when I see them. You love their cacophony. Their quick eyes.

I've never told you, but I loved a boy once. Loved him for his dark skin and the sadness of his eyes and for the way he dug his fingers into me when he held me. He was also from here and knew the sounds of all the birds. He taught me their names, their cries, their songs. Not just owls and crows but *palomas* and *urracas* and *golondrinas* and *garzas* and *ruiseñores* and *chachalacas* and *cenzontles*. He taught me the silhouettes of golden eagles and vultures, road runners and bobwhite quails by tracing them over and over on my skin. I hardly had to say his name, Abel. I'd just cry out like a grackle the way he'd taught me, and he'd turn to look at me.

We met the very first week of our first semester in college. I didn't tell my family about him. He didn't tell his family about me. Before he ever said the word "love," he said, "If they knew, my brothers would fight over who'd put the bullet between my eyes." Neither of us went home for Christmas break. His family in Texas and my family in Nebraska were too far and too poor for them to come visit. Spring came and went. Our last night together, he wept in my arms. I called him every day that summer, left messages with a woman who only spoke Spanish. He never called me back. Eventually, she started to hang up when she'd hear my voice and then the number was disconnected. When fall came, I went back but he didn't. I couldn't sleep. I'd wake up screaming, wake up calling for him. With time, the silence froze something inside me, but the bird songs stayed with me. I took to staring out an open window, even when winter came, even when the temperature dropped below freezing and there were hardly any birds in the sky.

It was because of him that I learned to love you. I knew your name before I ever spoke to you. Had seen you in class a dozen times, seen you talking to your friends, seen you across the room at a party or two. I'd even thought you had beautiful eyes. But I'd never talked to you. Until the day I passed by you with your friends and heard you describing the *urracas* you loved, how they swarmed and flipped and wheeled in the sky above the grocery store parking lots back home. Thousands every evening. All those splintered wings and their deafening sound. Your voice was filled with such longing. Later that afternoon, you were sitting alone at one of the cafes on campus. I decided to approach you, ask you something about a class assignment. We ended up deciding to meet over pizza to talk about our papers. We shut the place down, I walked you back to your building and then walked home in a daze.

Since then, my heart has belonged to you only. But that first night in South Texas, when you were introducing me to your parents, I heard the *cenzontles*, and they made me think of him and I felt a little less like a stranger. I knew the names of the birds. Their songs already lived in my bones. And I knew your home could be mine.

I graduated but stayed with you because I refused to risk what we had to distance. I worked until you graduated too. We moved to California while you went to med school. I worked while you studied. And then the pull of the Texas border became too much.

I'd lived with the whispering for a while before I thought to mention it to you. We were sipping coffee with our *pan dulce*, both of us reading at the kitchen table. You lifted your head up for a second, tilted it like a bird and gave me an odd look. You turned away without saying anything. I knew what it meant when your face turned to stone and your silence swallowed everything. There were things you wouldn't discuss, and if I insisted, you'd go to the small unadorned room farthest from our bedroom. You'd said it'd be your hobby room and double as a guest bedroom, but it didn't even have a bed in it. Just a single chair. The first time I found you there, your eyes were closed and you were silent, shaking and shaking in that chair.

I didn't bring up the whispering again, even when it started to follow me everywhere. For the first few years, I only paid attention to it at night when I was alone. It followed me to work and when I went jogging and when I ran errands. It was there when I was with you, growing so loud I could hear it even when we were with your family—the cacophony of voices, music, tv, children and pets unable to drown it out entirely.

I started driving at night when the whispering stopped being whispering and became distinct voices. Men and women and children. Sad, angry, happy, lonely, lost, demanding. In English and Spanish and languages whose names I didn't know. Sometimes it seemed like they were praying. Reminiscing. Weeping or laughing or screaming or whimpering or calling out for someone who never answered. Sometimes I can barely understand what they're saying, but the voices grow louder and then fade and then grow louder again. And sometimes I go suddenly deaf—the voices and all the sounds of the world gone. And it feels as if my insides have been scraped at, leaving parts of me raw that should never be touched.

I haven't spoken to them. I don't even know if they know I can hear them. I imagine it would be worse if they were trying to get my attention. If every plaintive cry began with, "Antonio, Antonio." Almost every night, I drive, keeping my eyes on the road, letting the wind and the music drown out the voices. I drive until I'm so exhausted I sleep even with all their voices booming and ricocheting inside my head.

I'm not imagining them. I'm not losing my mind. They're real. I've never heard the voices of the dead before but I know that's what they are. I want to tell them they have the wrong guy. They're not my ancestors. My family never passed through here. Not this land, not this river, not these roads, not even this sky. Why choose me when they could choose one of their own? Someone born and nurtured on this land, someone taught to speak sing pray here? I don't know what they want. They're not asking for my help. They just gather around me as if they're moths, and I'm giving off some light I don't know how to turn off.

I have deaths curled inside me. Layered and limned with my grief. I lost my mother when I was little, my brother soon after I met you, my grandparents after we married, some friends and, now too, our daughter. None of your people have died. Your parents, your grandparents, your great-grandparents, all your sisters and brothers are still living.

I know our daughter was your first death. But you won't call it that. Never born, you said, only sixteen weeks. As if that wasn't enough time to start thinking of names, to imagine how she'd have your water-straight hair and your dimples. "Socorro," I'd breathed against your barely rounded belly. Before you told me, I'd dreamt of a little girl riding on my shoulders, a little girl with my mother's name. I heard her laughter and felt her tiny hands in mine.

I dream her all the time. Small enough to fit inside the palm of my hand—my little ruby-hearted girl. Perfect tiny limbs, fingers, toes. Her little belly. Her little arms. I wait, breathless, to see her eyes open, but they never do. Her flesh a rosy color. The tremendous pulse of her heart pulsing through her entire body. Sometimes I look for her when I'm awake. I get lost in our house wondering why I can't find the nursery. I wake up thinking I hear her crying.

You won't speak of it. I've never seen you cry. But sometimes something moves over your face that reminds me of the ocean, and I know you're thinking of her. If I stay silent, you'll stay in the kitchen but move to stand by the sink. Your mourning place. You keep your face turned away from me. And if I stand behind you and wrap my arms around you, you'll lean against me but push my arms up so that they are wrapped around your shoulders instead of your waist. It doesn't matter. I'm here if the day comes that you need to cry. I'm here even if that day never comes.

The first time we made love, I tasted my own tears on your skin. I didn't know who else to go to when they called to say my brother had died. A car accident. No alcohol, no drugs, he just took the curve too fast and spun out of control. No seatbelt. Died instantly when he burst through the windshield. My little brother Armando gone, just like that.

Tears were streaming down my face when I knocked on your door. You led me to sit on your bed, then crawled into my lap and wrapped your arms and legs around me while I sobbed into your neck. Even now, all these years later, when my lips are on your skin, I can still taste those tears. Or perhaps I am tasting yours, all the tears you've never released, restless oceans pushing up against the surface of you.

It would have been simpler if I could have convinced you when the voices were only whispers. Or when it was only voices, because then I started to see their faces in my dreams. And then when I was awake. Shadows inhabiting all reflective surfaces. The bathroom mirror, the kitchen stove, my coffee mug, the car windshield, storefronts, anywhere, everywhere. All of them strangers. Sometimes they seemed to be looking at me. I learned to ignore them, learned to avoid focusing on their eyes, their mouths.

I went with you because it was your family's tradition to go to the shrine in San Juan on Sundays. We arrived first and waited on the sidewalk until your parents and grandparents and siblings and cousins arrived. There were hugs and kisses and handshakes and shoulder thumps in greeting. At least thirty of us when we started walking toward the shrine. Palm trees and oak trees and acres of green grass. Concrete beds of overflowing flowers. It was always beautiful and grand. I would have preferred the outside grotto at the San Juditas Tadeo church that you and I went to when we wanted to pray, but your family preferred to get dressed up and come to the shrine. I kept you close to me, my hand spread across your back, my thumb touching your bare skin. The sight, scent, touch, taste of you made the voices recede. I didn't know why it worked that way. If it was because you didn't believe in such things, if it was because you dealt with life and death every day, if it was because we had always been each other's refuge.

I took your hand as we climbed up the steps. You gave me a worried glance when the first step inside the building sent a jolt through my entire body. I held your hand too tightly, but I managed to nod. You seemed reassured. The sound of trumpets, violins, guitars and *guitarrones* filled the altar space and then rose in a wave toward us. The music sent the voices colliding into each other, rendering their words unintelligible. We took our seats in the pew. An intense brightness filled my sight, until I couldn't tell where one thing ended and another began. The line of mariachis became one blur of blue with shining metallic streaks. The priest's face and hands merged with his robes. Even the Virgen de San Juan on the wall—the blue of her dress wavered, as if it were water reflecting sunlight rather than wood and turquoise paint.

Only her face was as I remembered it, dark and serene. Her eyes black and radiant. When it was time to kneel, I looked to her, looked only to her and prayed with my heart in my throat: Milagrosa, make it stop. I can't do this. One man can't contain all of this. Can't channel it. I will lose my mind if this goes on much longer. What do I do, Virgencita? Any moment now, they'll learn my name and then their voices will never stop. I can barely sleep. Barely work. All I hear is them. I am not strong enough to bear this. To hear them. To carry them. Help me. Please help me.

The voices and all the colors came crashing back as soon as we stepped through the doors of the shrine. I put both hands to my head, unable to take another step. Spikes of pain. You wrapped your arms around me as if you feared I was dizzy. I heard your parents saying my name. You made our apologies and took me home. I leaned my head back and closed my eyes, the voices too close, too urgent when you weren't touching me.

The house was dark and cool. You put my arm over your shoulders and took me to our bedroom. I shrugged off my guayabera after you unbuttoned it. Took off my undershirt. Shoes and pants. Lay down on top of the comforter in my boxers. You were gone for a second but then came back with a cool compress for my eyes.

I took hold of your wrist, "Don't go away, lie down with me." I heard you slip off the strappy sandals and the salmon pink dress you'd worn. Earrings and bracelets and rings clacking onto the nightstand. I sighed when you lay down on your side against me, and I felt the long bare expanse of your skin. The voices gentled.

"Antonio, what's wrong? What's happening?"

It wasn't the time to tell you. It was too late. There was too much and too little to tell. It would have been different if you'd asked me when it was just whispering.

"Just let me hold you, Raquel. I feel better when I hold you."

I kissed your temple, and you sighed when I pulled you on top of me, wanting to feel not just your skin but your weight on me. So that I could pretend you'd never leave our bed. That I would spend the rest of my life like this, your body on mine holding the voices at bay.

I slept for the first time in days. When I awoke, you'd already left the bed. We had dinner, your eyes dark and worried the whole time. I didn't know what to tell you. The voices were too loud and the light was so bright, I kept wincing. Before you left to the hospital, you brought me a glass of water and painkillers. "We're talking about this when I get back, Antonio." You shrugged with one last helpless look before you picked up your keys and opened the door to the garage.

I don't know if I slept or not. If it was one hour or many. The bathroom mirror showed me a man with swollen eyes. Beard stubble. Sweat drenched hair. Alone with the voices. With the faces. They kept whispering my name. Over and over, in looping chains, so that the O at the end merged with the A at the beginning, creating a new name for me. A name without end.

I shoved on my sneakers and headed to the garage, passing by the kitchen counter where a single religious candle burned. The Virgen de San Juan. I touched the cool base, watching the light flicker and flare across the dark room. I remembered my prayer, the blurring colors, the sharp pain I'd felt. I leaned forward to read the prayer on the back, but the only words I could distinguish were "the Way of Life which gives meaning to moments of sorrow." There's always a candle burning on the counter, a second one always lit before the first goes dark.

The voices left me unable to think, but it had all become habit. Car door. Ignition. Garage door. Windows down to let the hot air out. Warm wind poured in. I didn't know where I was going. I just wanted to go fast. Fast so that the wind was louder than their voices. A few turns and a couple of miles between our quiet neighborhood and Highway 107. I saw their faces everywhere I looked, under the streetlights, in the headlights of oncoming traffic, in the rearview mirror. I refused to look at them, didn't want to see their mouths shaping my name: "Antonioantonioantonioan …"

I'm not in Edinburg anymore. It's dark out here. My foot presses harder on the gas pedal. The radio seems louder, all fluttering accordions and rolling drums. Other towns pass in quick-lit blurs. I stop reading the city limit signs. I turn and turn and turn on impulse. I stop reading the signs that tell me how many miles it is to San Antonio. How many miles to South Padre. North. South. East. West. One and then the other and the other. Where I go doesn't matter, only that I *go*. I don't want the city, and I'm not going to the beach. That much I know. It's not the ocean I want tonight. The night smells different now—more earth, more green. Finally, it's cool enough that the earth has begun to release the day's heat. The scent is what life would smell like if life didn't depend on blood.

The voices are getting louder. I turn up the radio. I barely brake turning onto a caliche road. Don't slow down even though the road is uneven and narrow. I want the wind to tear me away. I imagine a cyclone whirling on the road, tossing up me and the car and all the faces, all of us spinning and spinning until we're flung away from each other and into the silent sky.

I hear it right away—the small sound. Much softer than the voices, the wind, the music. It's not calling my name, but I know it's meant for me. It's mine. It's so dark here, it's hard to make out where the turnaround is. Barely enough reflectors to keep the tires off the grass. And then I floor it. As fast as I can go, following the soft sound. Sometimes I think I see animals in the shadows. Sometimes I see people, their faces too bright, surprised by my headlights at this hour of the night. The city limit signs come and go again. If I'm thirsty or hungry, I don't feel it. If I was tired or sleepy, that's gone too. I'm listening as hard as I can, entering the ramp for the freeway, swerving around eighteen wheelers and cars and pickup trucks.

It's not as if I'm responding to my name. Or your voice. It's almost like something I felt in those first delirious months of falling in love with you. As if I could feel you thinking of me when we were apart. As if something of me was twisting and pulling against something of you. That's what this was. A pull on my insides, as if something was threatening to unravel if I didn't listen, didn't respond, didn't follow.

The wind was changing. A slight coolness. The scent of sweet green things. I pull over on the side of the road by brush and mesquites. Hope that my car doesn't draw the attention of the Border Patrol. I walk in the dark. For a long time, constantly scanning every direction. But there's no one to stop me. Only one light on the sign at the entrance. No security. My feet know the way. I've been here a hundred times. Raquel and I were here only a few weeks ago, protesting the wall they want to build here. The wall that will desecrate one of the last few wild places. The branches of the trees move serenely in the wind, as they have moved, undisturbed, all their lives. Even though there's hardly any light, the little neon orange flags marking a line on the ground are as obscene as they are in full daylight. I fall on my hands and knees—the voices swirling around me—and start pulling the flags out of the ground. The earth is soft beneath me. The earth is solid beneath me. I can hear the river. Smell it. The trees are wide shadows, more alive than I am. But I know what's possible. Remember how horrified I was the first time I saw the endless concrete of the California-Mexico border. San Diego so green and so blue and then the roads to Tijuana and the shock of towering walls—the earth burned, razed, salted. Pale dead earth as far as the eye could see. The lights. The Border Patrol trucks. The uniformed men with guns.

Here in this natural place there is no concrete. There are no walls. Only these little orange flags marking death, death, death. In this darkness, I can't see the faces, but the voices are growing louder. You can feel it here, a shuddering under the skin. How the river here connects to the river everywhere. How the river carries hopes and dreams and losses and anguish. How the river is both water and blood. How the earth here weeps and sings at the same time. How it longs to be like the quiet earth elsewhere. And I understood that the voices were telling their own stories and the stories they'd been trusted with and the stories of this land that no longer had a voice to speak them. And my story was one of those stories. The faces had been witnessing, telling my story, braiding my story into all the stories that lived in this earth, connecting me, making me theirs.

There's a sudden dip I don't see in enough time and I go sprawling. End up on my back and only realize when I see the blurring stars that I'm sobbing. I couldn't hear myself over the voices. Couldn't feel my chest with the flags in my hands. The voices sound like they're sobbing too, but it's only my name, on loop, on loop, on loop, drumming at my temples.

The small sound is constant.
And then the wind stops. And then the voices stop.
  Completely. They stop completely.
I am alone.
No, not alone.

It wasn't fog that had slowly crept toward me but a mass of shadowed figures. There was the rushing of wings and the silhouettes of birds in flight. And the soft sound, louder now that the voices were gone. I could feel it under my skin. I wiped at my eyes with both hands and knew I was streaking my face with dirt.

He was whistling the song of the *golondrinas* and cradling something I couldn't see. My eyes were busy devouring his face. He looked exactly as I remembered him, hardly a day older. He smiled at me the way he used to smile at me, his eyes crinkling the way they'd always crinkled.

"Abel," I breathed.

He was so close, impossibly close. And I closed my eyes the way I'd always closed them when he was close. His lips on mine. Impossibly light. Impossibly soft. And I leaned into him the way I'd always leaned into him.

"Antonio," he whispered, drawing back. "Here, I've been taking care of her for you."

And the small sound filled me. She wasn't crying, wasn't whimpering. She was humming. She was so tiny in my hands. As beautiful as she'd been in my dreams. My little ruby-hearted girl. She opened her eyes. As wise and black as yours. Her little hand tried to grasp my fingertip. I held her up to my cheek, humming the lullaby my mother had hummed to me. And the small sound became a large sound, a thunderous sound. Her body, tiny and powerful, rumbled with it. And my hands warmed and started to radiate a golden light. And even in the blanket she was swaddled in, I could see her ruby light flashing like a jewel through her skin. Her heart beating fast like a hummingbird's.

I don't know how long I stood there holding her and looking into her black eyes. It was still dark when I heard Abel's voice again.

His voice was soft. "Come back whenever you want. We've been telling your story. Your mother and brother are almost here."

I stared at him. He held out his hands. I didn't want to give her back, but I knew we were running out of time. He held her delicately, reverently, as the light of her dimmed.

"One of us will always be waiting here for you. We'll teach you how to live with the voices."

In the night, the birds wheeling around us were almost silent. I stood there, watched their shadows draw away, watched the darkness lighten bit by bit.

The voices returned, but this time I didn't fight them. Somehow, though they were still loud, it no longer hurt. I walked and walked. Trying to understand what it meant to let them in, to let them flow through me, to feel like I was walking with one foot in this world and the other in theirs. Soft earth, soft light, soft river. And underneath it all, the small sound. Alive in me.

It's okay, Raquel. I can tell you everything now. Or at least, as much as you can bear to listen to. I know what I am now. I am a bridge. The voices will always be with me. And it will be my work to listen to them—while I work, while I live, while I love you, while life moves forward. And when you're ready to see our Socorro, I'll bring you here.

There's nothing to fear. Everything is here. Abel. Our little ruby-hearted girl. Soon, my mother and my brother and all my lost ones. Here among the wind and the trees and the river. The voices and the light and the humming. And the birds. All the birds.

the seedling wife

Claudia

I was fifteen the first time I felt death. I had no language for it. It was an echo, a tremor in my bones. They said, "cancer," and I thought I would die. But it wasn't my death I felt approaching. All those nights I slept in a hospital, I felt things, heard things, knew things. I was never surprised when the next day brought weeping. Distraught mothers. Frightened children. Heartbroken wives. Eventually, I left the hospital. Eventually, they said, "remission." Eventually, the quiet returned and my bones stilled.

Until the air began to vibrate around my mother and didn't stop until she was in the ground. And then with others. Many others. I was never wrong. I could feel their last breaths gathering weeks before they were gone. I felt what remained in houses where someone had died. I stayed far away from cemeteries and hospitals. As soon as I realized that there were places where the ground didn't throb with the blood of the lost, I moved away from the border.

"Noxochitzin," I murmur against your hair. You hear nothing, because even in your sleep, you are never completely silent. Always murmuring, as if a river running south or a broad-leafed tree swaying in the wind or a rainstorm greeting the spring lived inside you.

The years do nothing to dull my desire for you. I ache for the scent of you, the feel of you, the heat of you. The softness and the firmness of you. The fullness and the hollows of you and the sweet and salt of you. There is nothing like the sound of my name on your lips.

Ameyalli

The thunder woke me. It hardly took a second to register your arm around me, your soft snoring. You're so still against me, unlike yesterday.

It was thundering then too. The still air and the heavy clouds and the light drawn tight and tense told me rain was coming. I took your hand and drew you away from your garden shed and pulled you down with me to the ground because I wanted you to feel the thunder rippling through the earth. Wanted for your flesh to hum against mine as the earth hummed against the both of us.

Lightning branched across the sky and there was a boom of thunder almost simultaneous with the light that lingered behind our eyelids. Darkness descended—darkness too heavy for day—and then the rain came, stinging and sharp against my skin. I covered your body with my own and then I was brushing against your lips and you exhaled hot hot, and your hands were strong on my hips and you made that low guttural sound in your throat that also felt like thunder.

Rain in my eyes, rain on my face, rain in my mouth against your mouth. Your hands firm against my back, on my waist, kneading my thighs, and your hands didn't stop, didn't withdraw, didn't soften. Your hands were on me and my face was against your neck and my mouth was panting against your skin.

You unbuttoned my jeans. Shoved them down enough to slip your hand against me, inside me. My body bucked against you and your mouth was on my throat and my hands were clawing into the earth. You withdrew your hand and used your whole body to push me to the ground beneath you, and I tasted the rain on your cheek. You tried to pull my wet jeans off until we collapsed in laughter and I had to help you, our mouths filling with rain. Cool green grass against my bare thighs, my hips, my backside. You knelt between my legs, and we pulled our shirts off at the same time, colliding, flesh against flesh. Warmth of you against me.

And, oh, the wild sweetness of your kisses, and the muscle of your arms and thighs under my hands. And the softness of your breasts, your belly, the insides of your thighs. You gasped then grunted as I bit at your collarbone, your ribs, your hipbones. Rain and thunder and the smell of the earth and my body and yours undulating against each other. Your face on my thighs and mine on yours and our mouths sipping and tasting and sucking. I spiraled and thundered and crashed and I could hardly concentrate but the taste of you was so and the feel of you was so and the heat of you was so and I felt your body shuddering and I could not stop. We cried out together and as we collapsed, shivering still, and the rain falling still, I thought I smelled flowers. We lay there, breathing and breathing and breathing.

This morning, I went to bring in the clothes we'd left scattered on the grass and saw that where we'd lain, full-grown lilies had sprouted in profusion everywhere, already blooming, the white and gold and pink and peach and tangerine and scarlet of Easter lilies and Asiatic lilies, of Sonatas and Sumatras and Stargazers.

Claudia

I woke and the seedlings were cool against my skin. Tiny roots raking my legs, my arms, my face. I woke and my hand was in the space between your navel and your hip. The tiny red leaves of a Japanese maple were curled against my thumb. There was a tiny sound as I lifted it up and pulled it away from you. I laid it in the shallow basin we keep on the nightstand with an inch of water in it.

You shifted in your sleep, turning onto your stomach. From the back of your knees, I pulled the leafless twigs that would become a Texas redbud. You didn't move. I brushed the dark hair away from your face, felt the raspy green of Arizona cypresses behind your ear before I saw them. One. Two. Three. Four of them in your hair. I ran my hand down the center of your back. Without waking, you turned back toward me.

That's when I saw it. It must have begun unfurling before we fell asleep. Six leaves, green, rounded but slender, glossy. A lime seedling. The first of its kind. In all my years with you, you'd never released a lime seedling. Its roots reached from your neck to the corner of your right eye. As if tears had pooled in the hollow of your neck. Grown solid, grown green, grown into leaves. When I pulled it away, it released the scent of sweet, wet earth. I dug my face into your neck, breathed you in. Tightened my arms around you, sighed and fell asleep again.

Ameyalli

I don't know what alchemies you perform. Only that every morning while I am making coffee, you take the seedlings out to your workstation beside the deck. Sift soil and sort the tiny pots. There are shelves and shelves and bins and bags with different kinds of soil, with river pebbles and sand and moss and bark and perlite and other things I still can't name. No moments of hesitation, no wasted movements. You find each seedling its best home, placing each one in the sunlight with care, breathing on each one as if you were kissing me. Even watering them, you are tender and careful, as if you wish you could be the morning dew.

In our first years, I thought you would tire of me, tire of them, tire of all the work—this work of plucking and sorting and potting and watering and weeding and sunning and growing and feeding and planting and tending. But you are as delighted now as you were then and you emanate peace as if you were the earth itself, breathing in the sunlight.

Claudia

To love leafing things is to know how life flows into death and back again. How many seeds have I planted and never seen emerge from the ground. How many tiny green limbs lost to the sun. Lost to cold and frost. Lost to darkness. Lost to too much or not enough water. Lost to pests. Lost to bitter soil. Lost for no discernible reason. Each green life that flourishes eases the ache of those that were lost. The ache of all the tiny, yellowed things I held in my hands. Shriveled and brittle and breakable.

But every budding flower, every unfurling leaf, every new green-tipped limb is a whole new miracle. From earth and sun and rain, they make and re-make themselves. It seems impossible. The journey from leaf to seedling to tree. Incandescent. All the green life furiously alight. Death kept at bay.

This is what you are. Sunshine in my hands.

It's impossible to count four hundred rabbits, but I know that's who they are. All of them white and slightly iridescent. Their eyes look at me intelligently. They possess no fear. They came in ones and twos at first. Then in threes and fours. They come into our yard at dusk, emerging from the magueys that grow along the east side of the backyard. Sometimes the magueys are there, the flower spikes unbearably tall, twenty feet high and more. Sometimes the magueys are only shadows.

I created a second garden just for them. Right at the very edge of our yard. Where the grass gives way to the woods. I planted everything they seemed to like most there. I don't know when it came to me that they were your brothers. They give me a solemn look, knowing that I watch them as they emerge from and return to the magueys as if the magueys were a doorway to another world. Sometimes they call me sister-in-love. All their ears twitched furiously the one time I was brave enough to say the names of your real mother and father. When I asked the four hundred rabbits, they told me you were what the old gods chose to make when they decided to make something new.

Ameyalli

The first time it happened, I didn't know what to do. I was only thirteen. First, there was the hint of red in the water streaming from my body in the shower. I touched myself and thought it was so strange to bleed and yet not hurt. And then I felt tiny leaves brush against my hand, and a sharpness pricked my fingers. I reached in further, took a hold of it gingerly and pulled it slightly. It didn't come free. I pulled harder. Panicked a little bit. But finally it came away from my body. I wasn't sure what it was, but the leaves looked like the leaves on the trees we had had in the backyard. So green, so green. The roots were twice as long as the little tree. A baby mesquite.

I didn't know what to do with it. I wrapped it in a hand towel and put it in my backpack. On my way to school, I tossed it into the creek when I passed over the bridge. Every morning, a single new seedling tossed into the creek.

Until the morning that there were three. The night before, I'd made myself come for the very first time. My friends and I had whispered about it, I'd read about it, had even talked to my mom about it, but I knew somehow that my body was different. I tried so many things, tried touching myself soft and hard, quick and slow, here and then there, tried fingers inside. Tried thinking, not thinking, and finally it happened. Like nothing I could have imagined. Leaves and roots erupted from my body.

The next morning I found three seedlings instead of one. Other times there were two or four. Every morning I launched them into the creek. On weekends I rode my bike and found somewhere to leave some of the seedlings. So many different kinds, sometimes in my hair, from the corner of my eyes, from my nostrils, my lips, my underarms, my navel, my hips, my thighs, from between my legs, from behind my knees, from behind my ears. Most of the time, I didn't know what they were called or where they were from or what they needed. I just knew I couldn't keep them. Knew my mother would ask me questions I couldn't answer.

I learned to lock my door at night and to search my body first thing every morning. It was hardest my first year in college when I had a roommate. I learned to wear concealing pajamas, to always sleep under covers, to wake several times in the night to check myself. I never allowed anyone to fall asleep in my bed, and with every lover, I feared a seedling would emerge and leaf under their hands. I was afraid to see fear in their eyes, and it wasn't long before that fear turned my body inwards. Blunted my desire.

Claudia

Sometimes it feels like I've spent my entire life waiting to hear that word again. The doctors are oddly careful. They won't say it. They'll say, "No signs of reoccurrence." Strangely, I believed them more when the tests were more invasive. What they do now, decades later, is too easy, too quick.

I don't know what I'd do if you weren't there holding my hand. If you weren't there to stay up with me the nights before I go in for the results. If you weren't there the nights I wake up gasping for air. And I tell you my dreams. I'm in the shower, always in the shower, running my hands over myself, checking for lumps and tenderness and worrying over the flesh that in its fifties is no longer as smooth as it once was. I feel a small bulge in my side and press my right hand over it. It throbs under my fingers, and then I'm holding it with both hands as it pushes and pushes. And I can feel my insides being overrun, my organs swallowed, and it grows and grows while the rest of me crumbles. And no one hears my cries and no one can help me.

I wake up because you're calling my name. You're already pressed against me, kissing my wrists, the palms of my hands.

Ameyalli

It's not enough to thank you. And I know I can't ever really know what it costs you. But I'm grateful. And my parents are grateful. And of course, they're grateful too.

Mom and Dad started taking me with them when I was ten or eleven. They wanted to teach me that action was necessary, that compassion was never wasted. We worked with a group of people that left water and food and clothing along the border. They wanted no more deaths. Each life saved was a victory. They'd seen too many dead bodies, starved and desiccated, killed by thirst, hunger and the heat of the sun.

For years, we hardly saw anyone when we were out there. And then you and I went to visit my parents on the border. You came with us. That changed everything. We learned to go where you told us to go. You'd tilt your head to the side, with that faraway look in your eyes and your hands clenching into fists. How many did we save once you joined us, arriving when things were at their most desperate.

Your Spanish is like mine. Like my parents'. North of the border Spanish. Enough to make ourselves understood. But we could speak to them and help them. Though sometimes we had to say, "*Lo siento*," because we were too late.

Mom and Dad weren't too late for me. They've shown me the retama where they found me. Golden blooms falling in cascades. They said I was humming and smiling. Not starved, not thirsty. Lightly swaddled in the early morning heat. No signs of a mother or a father or other people. No diaper. No bottle. No toys. No name. Wrapped in a length of sky blue cotton.

Claudia

On a summer day so long ago, you took my hand when I asked you to dance. Our friend Leticia was throwing me a welcome-to-Austin party. Tons of food. *Sangría* and margaritas served by the pitcher. Cumbia and salsa and rock *en español* playing in the backyard. You were the first woman in Austin I asked to dance. The first and the last.

We danced. We laughed. We drank. I followed you back to your place. We talked till the sun rose, and when I kissed you, our mouths tasted like coffee and dawn. You were the most beautiful thing I'd ever seen. The morning light golden on your dark skin. Only traces of eyeliner and lipstick left after so many hours.

I woke before you and found the seedlings in your hair spread across my face. I didn't question them. I had tasted you. Earth after rain on my tongue. I'd smelled the green behind your ears, behind your knees. And the first time I made you come there were colors blooming in your eyes. Your skin itself sang *life life life* under my hands, under my lips.

When you woke and saw me, you smiled, then rose in a panic and rushed to the restroom. I caught your arm, waved toward the seedlings I'd placed on the nightstand.

"It's okay. I'll take care of them. Come back to bed."

Your eyes were wide and you bit your lip, but you came back to me.

In that first week, only flowered trees were born from you. Small things. Barely more than twigs and roots and a leaf or two. I pored over the leaves, tracing their fragile edges with my fingers. In my mind, their future colors bloomed. The soft pinks of magnolias and redbuds, purple bauhinias and jacarandas and mountain laurels, blue paulownias, white manukas and dogwoods, yellow huizaches and retamas. All the fruits—orange trees and grapefruit trees and apple trees and peach trees. Crepe myrtles of every color. I plucked each one from you with wonder.

Morning sunshine streamed in from your bedroom window. I brought soil and bark and string. Made tiny baskets for each seedling, setting their roots in the soil and bark. I cut the string to different lengths, hung each seedling so that it would receive as much sunlight as possible. I wanted to delight you.

You cried and told me about all the seedlings you'd tossed in creeks and parks and other people's yards.

"Never again," I said, "I'll take care of them."

And I have. Trees grow slowly, but there are at least two hundred potted seedlings in our backyard at the moment. I've donated at least five hundred trees that were at least seven feet tall to local parks. There's a twenty-five mile stretch of highway outside of town that we supplied with native drought-hardy trees. Every now and then, I'll take a few into the forest and plant them where I think they'll flourish. I've dedicated twenty acres on the other side of the house to growing fruit trees.

All the time, I am surrounded by your leaves. Your flowers. Your fruit. Your seeds. Your scent.

Ameyalli

I've dreamt it, you know. I know what will happen the day I die. You'll need to stay close to me. You'll need to be there before I take my last breath. There won't be much time to carry me out to the empty land beyond the fruit orchards. In the moment I take my last breath, leaves will start emerging from every part of me, from every pore. Tendrils and branches. Leaves and blossoms and fruit and seeds. All my flesh, all my organs, ruthlessly rooting and seeding. You'll try but you won't be able to pluck them from me fast enough. They'll fall from my body and take root as soon as they touch the earth. You'll have to run, my love, you'll have to run as fast as you can. As soon as you lay me down, run. Without hesitating. It'll seem as if my body's exploding, entire tree trunks and branches bursting out of me. The green will spread in every direction so quickly that the earth will shudder and roll, heave and sigh. All of me, my eyes, my skin, my limbs, my blood converted into flowers, into vines, into a green river shot through with sunlight.

I've dreamt this, my love. I've dreamt this and your tears, but you'll never be alone. I'll always be with you. You can sleep among the roots of my trees. You can touch each blossom to your face and feel my kisses. You can eat any fruit and taste me. Live in my garden after I am gone.

It will take years, perhaps decades, but a strange flower will bloom. And you'll see a seed, pearl white, the size of your fist. Take it to the desert where I was found. Take it when you feel your days coming to an end. Embrace it and you'll be embracing me.

Claudia

Age hasn't slowed your parents down at all. They're flourishing in the heat, attending protests, registering voters, translating for refugees, fundraising for various nonprofits, still trekking out into the empty spaces to leave water and dry foods. I'll come along too and do what I can.

And then we'll come back here, our home, our garden, our little forest away from the city. To days and days with you. Nights where we have dinner on the patio and the candlelight causes the first few gray hairs on your head to glimmer like silver. Mornings when the first thing you say is my name. My hands will harvest the seedlings from your body. I'll wonder at how they emerge from your skin. How they multiply in number each time I make you come, again and again and again. And they're not always trees nowadays. I've been surprised by tiny orchids from your thighs, passionflower vines from your feet. I went to nibble at your neck and followed the scent of roses until I found them rooted behind your ears. I want to know what else your body will learn to make, what else will emerge. Will there be little succulents on your back, green thumb-sized balls of cactus on your legs, bougainvillea branching out of your hair? Will I see plants that have not grown in the Americas in centuries, in millennia?

We live in a paradise of our own making. We are still a long way from goodbyes, my *noxochitzin*. I hear no whispers in the wind. Today is not our last day. Tonight we'll sleep in each other's arms. And tomorrow morning, I'll find pots for the new seedlings.

in this dream of blue horses

there are no roads only undulating land in every direction only bodies beautiful and blue and lit by the moon only the slight coolness that night brings after the heat of the day only our sister wind our brother wind that both blow against us and carry us along

we were not born here but our mothers' mothers' mothers called this land their home the bones of our ancestors do not live in the first few feet of earth under our hooves but listen close listen close and you can hear the thundering of their hooves their bones a few feet deeper only a few feet deeper our mothers' mothers' mothers called this their land their home and the land says oh my long lost long legged children and we the long lost long legged children whimper mother mother mother to the earth

in this dream of blue horses we are returned to the land of our ancestors we are wild again but then did we ever lose our wildness we were only waiting and our children born free do not remember captivity they would call us feral but we were never truly domesticated we only bided our time none of us had to remember freedom or our stories or the structure of our families the knowledge was never taken from us we were only prisoners to the bit and the bridle and the saddle and the spur but our spirits were never anything but free and even then we dreamed and we dreamed and we ran and we ran

in this dream of blue horses in this dream that is our living our breathing our being we run as one all our bodies all our hooves all our hearts all our flared nostrils all the stretch and coil of the meat and muscle of us made one made a river under the light of the rising moon and the waning sun this was always our land this was always our freedom this was always our strength we thunder we thunder we thunder

of the green grasses

I was already there when she was given by the Chontal Maya of Potonchán to the Spaniards. They were as strange to her eyes as they were to mine. In her mind, I heard her remark on the paleness of their faces and the strangeness of their light-colored hair and the oddness of the metal covering every inch of their bodies. She told herself she would not betray any fear, that she would stand tall and very, very still. The women around her shivered and cried silently. At first, I did not understand that she was being given as a slave, as a tribute, as a spoil of battle. She refused to even think it as she was presented to Cortés. She did not lower her eyes as his fell upon her. I saw him through her eyes, felt her register his sudden stillness. His eyes and hers and mine flared simultaneously with a sudden piercing light. I shivered though I had no body to shiver with.

But she was given to someone else, one of Cortés' lieutenants, Alonso Hernández Portocarrero. I shuddered whenever he entered the tent. She never betrayed herself, not a single flinch, not a single tear—only the involuntary grunts that escaped the back of her throat. I could have shut myself away, closed myself off from what she experienced, but I stayed with her. I couldn't leave her to suffer alone. At the very least, I could share her pain and shed her tears. Hernández was careful never to touch her face or to leave visible bruising. The other women did not fare as well. A few of them had been given individually to some of Cortés' lieutenants. The others were used by all his men. They were bruised, often bloody, and never lifted their eyes.

I've inhabited other bodies, but none like this, with senses so close to my own. And even among my own people, I'd never felt this intense connection. I hadn't thought I'd explore this world in the body of a woman. In a body so much smaller than mine. Our peoples both have two legs, two arms, one head, similar nervous, digestive and reproductive systems, but there the similarities end. I didn't know I'd feel through her skin as I might feel through mine. I see and hear and taste and touch everything through her.

Her pain is my pain. Nightly, he grabs her from behind and pushes her face down into the rough mat she sleeps on. I want to scream. So does she, but she forces herself to remain silent, forces her body to remain still. This is blasphemy among my people. We do not even have a word for this violence upon the body. I cannot see his face. Is it slack with desire? Is it filled with rage? Blank with satisfaction? She is not a human to him, not even a body, only a thing to slake his need. She lies a moment on the floor where he leaves her. I am weeping for her because she will not let him see her pain. Or perhaps because she knows it is of no use. She curses his name with the taste of blood in her mouth.

She does not know my name. If she hears my voice, she does not understand my words. She never betrays my presence. But sometimes, in her sleep, she holds her own shoulders in her hands as if she is reaching for me. And in her sleep, she sighs when I wrap my long-furred arms around her. I do not forget why I have come to this world, but still, my flesh clings to hers, my eyes, my hands, my breath. It was not love. She simply became half of me, and I became half of her. There was no separating us.

I am the Dreamer of the Seventh Family of the Northern Circle. The youngest son, promised to the service of the Mother. I dreamt our cities in ruin, our people destroyed, our violet-colored blood soaking the ground. I was only a child when I was given this dream. Death and destruction night after night after night. Our world and our memory wiped clean.

I was taken to the Mother to relate my dream. She held me in her arms as I wept and my body shook. With her own hands she held warm tea to my lips. Afterwards, I was allowed to return to my nest family only twice a year for two seven-days. Otherwise, I remained in the capital, a student of the Five Elders. Trained in our people's stories, in dreaming, in mind-sharing, in the folding of time, in true seeing. And in my sixteenth year, without warning, I was reassigned. To prepare me, they said, for what the Mother had herself dreamt.

It was another four years before the Mother revealed her plan to us. I was one of two hundred. Half of all the dreamers under a certain age. I wept when I married my wife, knowing we would not grow old together. Wept when my children were born, knowing I would never see them grown. I was twenty-five when the Mother declared the ships were ready. Ten ships with twenty dreamers each. The morning we set out, I woke covered in sweat and with tears streaming down my face. We, the two hundred, made our farewells. We did not expect to ever return. I prayed as we left our planet's atmosphere. Prayed for a vision broader than my own. A wisdom greater than my own.

Guide my hands, I begged the Supernal Green. Guide my eyes, guide my tongue and guide my will.

Our mission was simple. Go out, find other worlds in the midst of devastating conquests. Live among them. Observe. Report every detail, no matter how seemingly trivial, to the Elders and the Mother. They would sift through alien histories and glean the wisdom to save our people.

I do not hope for victory, but I cannot surrender my hope of survival.

It took us a decade to come to this world. A decade of goodbyes, each dreamer pointing in their own direction in turn. When my turn came, I woke screaming. Left my bed to find the captain. At first I could do no more than point while I wept. Six galaxies away, I heard their cries and their resignation—they'd known death was coming. Their ruler's fear was such that he had the dreamers killed. He could not see their faces. Could not endure what they'd foretold.

I had not thought to find another people with their own dreamers. Dreamers with dreams that so closely mirrored my own. Inhabiting a blue planet, third from its sun.

Sleep was always difficult. For both Malinalli and me. Every night I laid awake for hours, even after Malinalli finally stilled and slept. I'd open my eyes and think of the night sky and its many stars. Maybe I only imagined it, the ever-present sense of knowing where my world was. As if I could reach in that direction and touch some part of it. Ten years since I'd said my goodbyes to my family, to my wife, to our two children. She'd chosen to be with me for whatever time we had, knowing the Mother intended me for a mission from which I would never return. And as much as it had hurt to take my leave of her, I'd never felt the pain I felt when I held my children's small bodies in my arms for the last time. But they were what had filled my heart with resolve. I left not just to save my world, my people. I left to save their lives, their world, too.

I know why I can't sleep. Even here, I still dream the end of my world. I dream the empty violet sky, bodies and rubble piled everywhere. Smoke and fire. All our cities razed to the ground. Some nights, I dream my children, their limbs terribly still. Every night I fall asleep against my will.

Those first days with Malinalli, I woke, always, to the flow of words. She practiced silently, shaping the Spanish words with her lips and tongue. She tasted them, rolled them on her tongue, bit into them. She kept long lists of words she felt she needed to know, and day by day, fit each new word into the space she had made for it. She listened to the Spaniards intently, all day, every day. The other women stayed to themselves, doing as they were bid or sitting still like stones. Her mind was never still, never silent. She wielded each word as if it was a weapon, learning its heft and its sharpness. I learned Cortés' language as she did, while learning from her the two languages she already knew. Her tongues came more naturally to me than this Spanish she was learning. Its structure was another level of alien.

There came a morning, when we were still camped by the river, when all the women were stripped and dressed in long white gowns. There was a strange Spaniard we had not seen before, dressed nothing like Cortés or his men. He waded into the water and looked up expectantly. They pulled Malinalli forward first. Some of the women screamed, perhaps fearing they were about to be drowned. The man in the water beckoned her to him. Showing no fear, she entered the water without having to be dragged in. He said something, but neither she nor I understood him. He spoke another tongue to her. At this, she leaned intently toward him and words flew back and forth. Later I learned the strange Spaniard was something called a "priest," the conduit between these Spaniards and their deity, and that he knew one of Malinalli's tongues. Malinalli spoke Mayan and Nahuatl. In time, Malinalli came to translate from the Nahuatl of the peoples around us to Mayan, and the priest translated the Mayan to Spanish for Cortés.

But that morning, I could not keep up with all the different languages being spoken. The Mayan was still mostly unknown to me, and I'd only begun to understand some Spanish. In her mind, I only heard flashes of language, knew that she consented before the priest laid his hands on her head and pushed her under the water. When she rose, he called out a new name. "Marina," he said, and she nodded her head. Only I heard her thoughts. "It does not matter what they call me. My name will always be Malinalli, of the green grasses."

More and more, Cortés kept her by his side. As her proficiency in Spanish grew, the priest was called upon less and less. Cortés had her possessions moved from Hernández' tent to his. I no longer spent the nights weeping for her. She and I spent the days watching Cortés, straining to hear his every word, register his every change in mood. He wielded the power of life and death over all of us, his moods were mercurial and his thoughts impossible to predict.

At the same time, there was what neither of us could explain, what neither of us tried to articulate, not even to ourselves. How the sound of his voice tumbled and ricocheted inside of us. How her body and mine moved unconsciously toward him whenever he was near. That same sense of lightning familiarity each time our eyes met. He stopped her breath. Otherwise, she betrayed nothing. Even without a body, I felt mine leaning toward him. Felt urgency and heat low within me. My desire and hers like kindling and flame, the desire to devour him and be devoured raging within us both. We waited, but he never reached to touch her.

Malinalli went to great measures to avoid Hernández. There was growing anger in his eyes every time he saw her. We were out of sight of everyone, bringing back water to Cortés' tent, when he stood in our path. Malinalli kept her gaze averted and turned to walk the other way.

"What, slave, now you are too high above me to look at me?"

Malinalli stood very still. By then, I knew her well enough to fear for what might happen next. She stared straight at him, her lips curling slightly.

He raised his hand and struck her. She fell to the ground, and before she could rise, he had covered her body with his, legs forcing their way between hers.

There was a sudden loud roar, and Hernández' body went flying. He quickly rolled to his feet and had his hand on his sword in seconds. His eyes widened when he saw that it was Cortés. Cortés did not say a single word, the eerie light in his eyes not entirely sane. Hernández turned his face and walked away.

Cortés touched her cheek. She stared up at him. I stared up at him.

He held out his hand and helped her rise to her feet. "Hernández is returning to our land. I will not let him take you with him. I will have you stay with me. Is that acceptable to you?"

"Do not pretend I have a choice. If I don't choose you, you will send me to another."

"Marina, I want you by my side. You will not want for anything, and I will treat you well, with gentleness and honor."

"What honor does a slave have? A slave has no choice. There is only being the slave of one man or another."

"You are a slave no longer. No one will ever raise a hand to you while I live. You will be addressed as Doña Marina. You will be my translator and adviser ... and my *compañera*, if you wish. Already you live in my tent. You have the proof of my words. I have not even attempted to touch you."

"Because I am of value to you. Because of me, you are moving through the land swiftly, the great and small leaders of the people bowing their heads to you. You and your men are growing rich without risking your lives."

"Yes, and I am not a fool. I will not let a gift of providence come to harm. For the rest, you decide. I will not bother you. Come to me as you wish. Or not."

She went. One night and then another and then another. She went though she often lay for hours under her own blankets and told herself not to rise up and meet him under his. I heard the doubts thundering through her mind. Life was uncertain. Who was she not to suck the marrow out of it? To take what pleasure she could find in it? What strange thing was it that she felt every time he looked at her? Every time she touched him? He was the Bringer of Devastation. The world was not what it had been. Better than anyone, she had the best vantage point to see how the world was being re-carved. She saw the maps Cortés pored over nightly. She saw the battles, heard the screams of all her dark-skinned people. He was touching her with hands steeped in blood. But what loyalty did she owe the people who had taken everything from her and given her to this alien, this Spaniard? My brain whirled with hers, all of her anguish echoing in my chest. And I wondered if, at that moment, my people were already dying or if my world was already gone.

She did not go to him alone. I went as well. Her will always stronger than mine. The longer she resisted, the louder the keening I could not hold back. Even without a body, I ached for him. I looked out through her eyes when he held his hand out to her. My hand also took his hand. My mouth also tasted him. My body also welcomed him into it. I sighed when she sighed. Moaned when she moaned. And I gave myself and she gave herself and he gave himself until there was only what the three of us together became.

I am not who I was when I first came to this world. I have learned too much. Seen too much. I had dreamt violence but never lived it this way, never been surrounded by it. So much blood. Fear. Pain. On my world, it had never been necessary to build walls, thick and high, around my heart. Never necessary to harden my soul, to let it callous over. This world made me something my people would never have recognized. It was necessary. Otherwise, I would have spent all my waking hours weeping. The violence would have corrupted my mind. And if my mind had gone, I would have freed my body—so much taller and stronger than these small creatures—and wreaked a more devastating destruction than they'd ever seen. My hands that had never known death would have created it, and my mouth that had never known the taste of blood would have torn at their flesh.

So I raised the walls and grew quiet. And distant. And learned not to feel all I felt. I learned to listen to her. Her thoughts. Her patience. Her will to survive.

Another night. Cortés had left us behind. Neither one of us could sleep. She'd run through all of her language drills. I'd meditated my daily report to the night sky and was wondering about my children when I heard her voice inside my head, inside her head.

"Who are you? What are you? You were not here before? I have heard you but did not know the meaning of your words. I have seen you, Cozamalotl."

"You have named me 'Rainbow'?"

"For your fur, for the way the light and the colors dance in it and above it."

"You can see me?"

"Yes, when I see my reflection, I often see yours. Sometimes I stay staring because I am lost in your eyes, their lustrous darkness, that thin circle of hot gold."

"Thank you for accepting me."

"Until now, I did not know I had. Though we could not speak, you made me feel less alone. You wept when I could not. You made me stronger. I did not mind sharing my language or my memories with you." She hesitated. "You know that I have seen your Dreams?"

"No, Malinalli, I did not know that."

"I see your people fallen, their bodies piled everywhere all the way to the horizon. I see your world burned, smoke rising, your homes and your temples razed to the ground. I hear weeping and screaming. The sky is a strange color. Is the sky always that shade of violet?"

"Yes, that is the sky of my home world."

"Except for the sky, that is the same Dream my cousin dreamt every night of his life."

"Was he at the massacre?"

"Yes, like so many others, called by the emperor to relate his Dream. Killed because the emperor could not bear to hear them all speak the same Dream. I dreamt him before we heard the news, and in my dream, he told me to be strong, because the time of devastation was coming. Survival was a narrow road, he said."

"Did you ever dream him again?"

"No, just the once. And when I saw the Spaniards, I knew it was the beginning."

I do not know what Cortés made of me. If he thought he imagined me. If he thought I was a demon or some strange thing borne of this new world he was intent on claiming. We were both "*Amor*" in his bed. Where his strength was greater than Malinalli's, mine eclipsed his. Those first nights, I never knew where Malinalli ended and where I began. Then a night came when I slipped out of Malinalli's skin, when I felt Cortés' hand on my skin and not on hers. He paused for an infinitesimal second, but then the lightning jumped between us and neither of us knew how to resist it. He held nothing back in the dark. There was no caution in him. He gave everything over. He didn't flinch when his body touched my fur. I swallowed his cries with my mouth. He trembled and shuddered under me, his body convulsing while I was still inside him."

Sometimes I watched him with Malinalli. Sometimes she watched me with him. Most nights it was the three of us, infinitely tangled, infinitely undone. It was never just Malinalli and me. The two of us were kindling. He was the spark.

"Tell me of your people, Cozamalotl. Do they live as we live? Are there slaves and warriors? Are they as different as we are from the Spaniards?"

"My world is very different, Malinalli. It is a peaceful world unified by the Mother."

"You have no battles? No wars? No nations? No slaves?"

"No, nothing like what I have seen of your world. The Elders tell ancient stories of strife, but I have never seen it or known it. My people live in cooperation. We are all empaths. To hurt others would mean hurting ourselves. We make art. We sing. We grow crops. We have families. We meditate. We learn the ways of the Elders. Our lives are long, much longer than yours."

"It sounds like a paradise. I can see why you would do anything to protect it."

"Anything, Malinalli, even make an exile of myself."

"And come to this mad world."

"If I can learn something here that will help my people survive, then I will have no regrets."

"Have there ever been conquerors on your world?"

"So long ago we have only one story: how The Wisest One of Us taught the First Song of Unity and linked minds for the first time. How this led to the defeat of the invaders we do not know."

"Sing to me, Cozamalotl. I would like to hear the songs of your world."

I sang her to sleep on the nights we were alone. The other nights, we spent with Cortés. On and on. Night after night of caresses and whispered things against his skin my fur her skin. Our bodies slipping in and out of each other. And during the days the campaign continued. We moved on, from one land to another. As I learned more of all the languages, I began to listen for the changes Malinalli made, how she softened and rearranged, praised and flattered. Where words failed, swords rose and the blood flowed into the earth, staining the rivers and the crops. Where language failed, the bodies piled up and burned. Where she failed, we were sent away while the soldiers meted out their fury. And sometimes Malinalli fell to her knees on the ground, begging for the end of blood. Sometimes Cortés listened. Sometimes he didn't. Difficult to reconcile the man who murmured sweetness in the night with the man who could command death without speaking a single word.

I was not entirely sure he was sane all the time. How could a man be wholly sane when he had set his ships on fire and told his men there was no return? A man who bathed in blood and dreamed of empire? A man who walked a land he had never known amid a people he had never seen and yet believed he could shape it into the world he'd left behind?

But those were thoughts that lived only in the daylight. I never thought of these things at night. Not when I was with them. Not when I touched them and they touched me. Not when I watched them with each other. We drank and drank from each other's mouths, drank our commingled scents, drank until our heads spun, until our bodies gave out, until we forgot each other's names, until we had no names.

But then Cholula happened. It wasn't an accident. Not an impulse. It was deliberate, executed step by step, and even I didn't understand until too late. It was Malinalli herself who damned the people of Cholula. She'd befriended one of the noblewomen who warned her to flee to safety before the attack. Malinalli reported the conspiracy to Cortés. The Tlaxcalans had become allies to the Spanish and traveled with us in great numbers.

"Our allies," Malinalli said.

"What, are you one of the Spanish now?" I'd asked her.

"They are our survival. Cortés is our survival. Without him, what becomes of me? Of us? And he is all the power I have in this life. Without him, I am a slave again."

"He is more than your master …."

"And more than yours too, Cozamalotl."

"And your people?"

"They all die without me. You have seen my dreams as I have seen yours. A world of ashes or a world of blood. There isn't an alternative."

"What if you are suffering only from a lack of imagination, Malinalli? Of faith?"

"Faith in what, Cozamalotl, what is there for me to have faith in? The gods? The gods did not prepare us for the Spanish. The gods did not stop the shedding of our blood. The gods are standing by, watching us die. There is nothing to have faith in but the swords of the Spanish."

"Tell me no untruths, Malinalli. You did this to save Cortés. Or to earn his trust."

"Cholula cannot succeed. They are foolish to think they can. They imagine that Cortés' men are all the Spanish that exist. It is not so. You have heard it from Cortés himself. There are multitudes in the world he comes from. More will follow. Always, more will follow."

"But your people ..."

"What 'your people,' Cozamalotl? They are not all my people."

"It is how the Spaniards see you. To them, all of you are savages, all of you are to be conquered. Killed."

"We are not like your people. We are neither a united people nor a united land."

"Then, may the Mother protect these lands and these peoples, Malinalli, because I do not see how any of you will outlive these times."

"Some of us will survive. I am determined, some of us will survive."

Cortés gathered all of Cholula in the square and accused them of treachery. The musket's sound boomed across the city, and then his men and the Tlaxcalans laid waste to every man, woman and child in the square. Malinalli stayed where Cortés had left her and watched the red blood of Cholula run.

I withdrew from her. I had nothing to say to her.

I meditated. Thought of the Mother until her face filled my whole mind. Bundled my thoughts and flung them toward Her. Waited for some tiny pulse of acknowledgment that it had been received. Nothing. Again, nothing. I prayed fervently in that moment. I prayed that the unity of my people would save them. I prayed that no would-be conqueror would divide us or turn us against each other. I prayed that no one of our kind would ever betray us. I prayed that there would be an end to these visions of blood spilling, red blood and violet blood.

Days later, I emerged and looked out of Malinalli's eyes. They'd begun without me. Cortés was in her mouth and then he was in mine, and his fingers dug into the longer tufts of fur at the base of my head. I looked up at him, wanting to hold him with my eyes the way I held him with my mouth. But it was neither the heat nor the tenderness in his gaze that seized my heart. I looked up at him and saw him covered in the violet blood of my people. Thought of him on my world with bodies piled all around him. Thought of him mercilessly spearing the children of my world. I heard their cries. I felt their terror, their pain, their anguish.

I choked on him, falling away from him and collapsing into Malinalli as I felt the bitterness rise in my throat, as I felt the need to convulse, to retch, to tear out my own mouth, to destroy myself for taking pleasure where I had taken it. I fled, further than I'd ever gone into the recesses of Malinalli's mind.

He did not call out for me, did not ask where I had gone, did not reach for me again. I felt Malinalli searching for me, but I withdrew more than I ever had before. Until I did not think she could feel me. I could not stand to be in my own skin. Or hers. I could not answer her, could not speak to her. Cortés was not the conqueror of my people. My people would never die at his hands. But in that moment, I could not bear Malinalli either. Her people and her world were dying at his hands. How was she able to let his hands touch her? So many times, in the midst of passion or afterwards, while resting against him or me, she would bite at his hands, suckle at his fingertips, kiss his wrists. As if she did not taste the blood or feel the death in his hands. I did not know if she could hear my thoughts. I wanted not to think anymore. I wanted not to be.

There followed a long period of darkness. I did not rise to the surface of her consciousness during that time. I could not bear to see any more killing. They were human bodies, but in those days, I could only see the bodies of my children, my people, lying in their spilt blood.

I could not understand how Malinalli could continue, not only to witness but to speak, to act. Until I found the iron wall of her will, the bedrock of her mind, which refused to give in to despair or madness. And I realized that she had no option to withdraw. She only had two choices: live or die. I had the luxury of a third: to hide.

And so, I hid. So deeply I did not even emerge to meditate my reports to the Mother. I could not. There was only weeping and screaming in my mind. In my days and nights, in my sleeping and waking, I could think only of my world and my people. Were they now dying as all of Malinalli's people were? Were they already dead? Was I sending my thoughts into the Void with no one on the other side to receive them? Had I traded my last few years with my family for nothing? Had the Mother sent us all on a mission merely for the sake of maintaining hope? I had known I would die without ever seeing any of them again, but I had not known how the time—how the years—would stretch and roll endlessly. It was one thing to sacrifice your life, another to live all of it on an alien world, in an alien body, never to return.

For a long while I did not answer when Malinalli called. For a long while I did not stir when I felt Cortés' hands running along Malinalli's body, searching for me. When I heard him call, "*Amor*," and know he meant me, not her. I was a body but not a body. I had no will to pull myself from Malinalli's flesh, to manifest myself in my own form. The Elders had warned against this. It was dangerous to let too much time lapse without materializing. It was only our force of will that allowed us to preserve the hold on our physical forms. To manifest them or disperse them as needed. But prolonged absences from our bodies made it possible to lose our bodies, to forget them.

I forgot to be afraid of forgetting my body. Of losing myself. Days and days and days passed. I did not care how many. Malinalli called for me without ceasing. That was all that tethered me, her voice, such a strong voice though it reached me only faintly in the well I'd fallen into. I didn't want to respond. I had nothing to say to her. I had nothing but the howling pain in my heart. The vision of my slaughtered family, my slaughtered people.

Then the night came when I couldn't turn away from her anymore. She was screaming my name. I rose to the surface, and her relief at hearing my voice shocked me. I could feel the tears in her eyes, tears I'd never seen her shed before.

All her thoughts swept through me at once. We were in Tenochtitlán. Cortés had returned from the coast. He had heard rumors that Governor Velázquez of Cuba had sent a large force to arrest him. While Cortés was gone, he had left Pedro de Alvarado in charge. The power had gone to his head. De Alvarado had ordered a massacre of nobles and priests, and not even Moctezuma had been able to calm the people's outrage.

Afterwards, the Spanish remembered it as the *Noche Triste*. Malinalli's mind was focused on surviving, nothing else. For myself, I did not care. It was not my sad night. I laughed and laughed, laughed without ceasing. Cortés gave them permission to carry away what they could. I laughed to see the Spanish killed by their own greed, fatally slowed by their desire to haul away gold. I laughed to see the Eagle Warriors rise. The old songs bubbled up in my throat, the ones my people no longer sang, the songs that we had sung in ancient battles. I laughed as we ran. I did not care if we lived or died. If we lived, there could only be more blood. If we died, I would rejoin my own kind, the energy of my life flowing back into the Supernal Green. I'd be united with all my loved ones, finally and forever at peace.

Malinalli chose not to respond to my howling laughter. She ran with the Spanish soldiers, ran for her life, away from the fires and the dying and the rage of Tenochtitlán. Into the night and over the river. And when we made it to what safety we could and I saw the tears in Cortés' eyes, I shrieked with laughter. Malinalli held him in her arms as he wept. She dressed his wounds, and I laughed to see his blood. Howled. While he slept, I emerged and licked his face, tasting the salt of his tears, and then dipped my head to lap up his blood with my tongue.

"Have you gone mad, Cozamalotl?"

"Yes, Malinalli, yes. Mad. I had not known … I needed to see the Spanish die. I needed to know they could die. I had begun to think it was not possible. I needed to see him weep, to see him bleed. I needed to taste it. Kiss me, Malinalli, taste his tears and his blood on my tongue. I will share them with you."

"We barely escaped with our lives …."

"This is the moment, Malinalli, we are alone with him, and he cannot protect himself. You see the knife among his things. This is the moment. Plunge it into his side. We will be free of him."

"Until they come to kill us …"

"Then we will die free, Malinalli. Come close, taste his blood on my lips."

"You have gone mad."

I laughed and I howled and I crumpled into a small pile inside her. We would never be free of him, I realized. Not while he lived. And not afterwards either.

I could not hide forever, and madness was not the refuge I'd hoped for. Not while the desperation of my people thrummed under my skin. I cursed myself the first night I went with her, the first night I went back to Cortés. The weakness of my people, to need touch, to crave it. In my whole life before this world, I had never slept alone. I'd never felt solitude as I felt it here, even though I lived within Malinalli. But I knew she would not understand me. She never looked back. Her childhood, the arrival of the Spanish, last year, last month, last week … they did not exist for her. She lived, always, in the present moment, and in preparation for the dangers of the future.

Outside of their arms, I could never forget my world, their world. Could never forget unless he was touching me. He had not fully recovered the night I returned to him, but he kissed every inch of me from the crown of my head to the bottoms of my feet, whispering his adoration over my skin, my fur, my eyes, my lips. I don't know how to describe what the need burning in his eyes did to me. It could make me forget. I think he made Malinalli forget. I think we made him forget.

We wouldn't have survived without each other. In time, the people came to speak of them as one person, one voice. They never knew me. I was the invisible third, bound up as inextricably as they were in the breaking and creating of the world. There was no better vantage point for me to observe, to report the unfolding of events to the Elders and the Mother. To endure my isolation, I needed them, their arms, our nights. I hesitate to think what Cortés and Malinalli would have become on their own.

In the year after the *Noche Triste*, Tenochtitlán, the glorious capital of the Aztecas, fell. While the Spanish rebuilt the city in their image, Cortés had a house built in Coyoacán for Malinalli to live in. We had servants. Blooming flowers and captive birds and a trickling fountain in the courtyard. Sometimes we could imagine that the world was peaceful, that Cortés was not extending his hold over the continent.

As the years passed, faster and faster, tears came more often. My world was often on my mind. I missed the violet sky, missed the almost electric green herds of clouds in the sky, missed seeing our two moons. Missed the mountains of my home. The scent of my world. The sight of my people. It became harder and harder to remember my parents' faces, my wife's hands, my children's voices.

I knew before Malinalli did that she was with child. Martín was a bright little light suddenly spinning before my eyes. I whispered songs and stories to him before he was born. Although she carried him within, Malinalli would not speak to the babe.

"The babe wonders at your silence, Malinalli."

"You know as well as I do, Cozamalotl, he does not belong to me. Of my blood, of my flesh, of my bone, but he will be his father's child, his only heir. One day Cortés will take him away to live in his world."

"He is still your son."

"Is he? He will be half of this land and half of that land. I will not try to keep him. It is best this way. He will never be torn from what he knows, what he loves. This child must be raised among his people, so that he will never feel like an outsider among them.

Martín was born early one morning. I was the one who cradled him until he fell asleep, the one who rose in the night when he cried out. Malinalli kept her distance. Martín had her eyes, dark and impenetrable, and his father's habit of curling his fingers in my fur when he slept. I loved him like he was mine. And he was mine. Born as much of my love as of theirs. I sang him the lullabies of my people, watched him breathe as he slept, brushed the silky hair away from his forehead.

A night came when I felt a presence and woke with a start. I'd fallen asleep with Martín on my chest. Malinalli was standing there, in the dark, her fingers lightly stroking Martín's rounded cheek.

"This life requires a heart of stone, Cozamalotl. I have never told you this, but my father loved me too much. My world ended when he died, and my mother gave me away. I have not wept since that day."

"Do you want to hold him?"

"No, if I hold him tonight, I will hold him again, and then it will hurt too much when it is time for him to go. I will let you love him for us both. The way you have wept for us both all these years. What little love I am capable of in this life, I give to Cortés." She laughed harshly.

Martín stirred. I rocked him gently until he calmed.

"I give it to a madman covered in blood."

I looked up at her, the only time I could not hold back the question that I'd bitten back a thousand times, "Why?"

Her eyes were deep, black as they'd ever been. "He was my only choice. The only choice I was ever given." She moved her hand, laid the palm flat on my chest next to Martín. "I do not love you, Cozamalotl. That is not what I call what you are to me. You are my very heart. All the love I possess you hold in your heart. You give it life. You give it faith. You give it hope. I can survive whatever happens, as long as you never leave me."

I held out my other arm, and she curled against my side. I held them both, mother and son, until the sun rose.

Cortés married Malinalli to a loyal man named Jaramillo. When the time came, Cortés took Martín away. I wept for us both, for myself and Malinalli. Martín was so little. Too little to remember me, but I knew his little heart would feel betrayed. I wouldn't be there when he was hungry or afraid or sleepy. Wouldn't be there to play with him or hold him or make him laugh. I prayed Cortés would find him a loving nursemaid. That he'd never cry himself to sleep calling for his "Coza."

Although Malinalli was married to Jaramillo, it was always understood by everyone that she belonged to Cortés first. Jaramillo did not even protest when we packed our things. Malinalli and I spent two years with Cortés during his campaigns in Honduras. It was very much like our first days again. I observed, listened, reported back to my world. I was often weary but not threatened with madness again. Afterwards, we went back to Jaramillo. Malinalli gave birth to a daughter. We kept her with us, although I could not tell you if she was Jaramillo's blood or Cortés'. She was Malinalli's, and that was all that mattered to me.

The last time we saw Cortés, it was 1530. Eleven years since we'd first met him. A few more lines on his face, a deeper darkness in his eyes. Malinalli's husband left her alone with him. We ran into his arms as if it was a homecoming, forgetting all our time apart. His hands on her hips as she leapt to wrap her legs around him. Pressing close behind him, I encircled them both with my arms. He leaned his head back, craning his neck to kiss me after he kissed her.

Later that night, our three bodies lay close, joined and separate. Malinalli was sleeping. Cortés was awake. He raised himself on one elbow and for the first time—his eyes clear and unclouded by passion—deliberately looked me in the eye.

"She calls you Cozamalotl, no?"

"Yes."

"What is your true name?"

"I do not expect you to be able to pronounce it, but I will tell you. It is _____."

"I don't know if I will ever see you again. I wanted to speak to you at least once like this. Wanted you to know that I knew you. That I knew you were no dream."

He leaned down and kissed me. Again and again and again. Then laid his face against my chest and breathed deeply of me until he fell asleep. I stayed awake. They both slept in my arms.

Years and more years. When Malinalli died, it felt as if half my body was torn from me. I have never stopped mourning her. Everything in this world reminds me of her.

I found another body to carry me and then another and then countless others. A year passed. A decade. A century. More centuries. I loved, many times, but never again like I had loved Malinalli and Cortés.

I travelled the continents, time and time again. I saw the deaths, the poverty, the oppression of Malinalli's people. Saw their numbers dwindle. I saw Malinalli's face on so many young women through the centuries. Nightly, I meditated and sent my reports back to my world. I lived centuries of despair and struggle and hope. Malinalli's people did not survive in their entirety, but they survived with enough intact to find their way back to themselves.

The new millennium was well into its third decade when I began to feel my days drawing to a close. By then, I'd been settled for close to seven decades in the place they called San Jose in the land of California. Everywhere there were signs of hope as I heard all the languages Malinalli had spoken spreading, all the stories she had told me being revived. The last two humans I chose to inhabit were both teachers and healers. I shared with them everything I could remember, everything I'd ever learned, everything I'd ever seen. There was a brightness in all their students. A light that shone inwards and downwards and outwards as they learned the words of their ancestors, tasted the medicines of their ancestors, danced as their ancestors had danced. There was a brightness in their eyes that made me want to weep. A brightness I'd never seen in Malinalli's eyes. A brightness that blood and conquest had dimmed in my memory.

And then I did weep, for Malinalli and for Cortés, for the broken world and the world returning, for all my centuries and my own lost world. I wept until my breath grew shallow. Until I knew the time had come to release my bodies, mine and the human one I'd decided would be my last. I did not know if my children or their mother still lived, but I embraced them in my heart, tried to remember their forgotten faces, hoped they had come to understand I had spent my life hoping my small efforts would help them survive.

I lay myself down and closed my eyes. It was time to return to the Mother.

the light of your body

My hands won't stop shaking. It was too quiet when I came home. Too quiet. And the quiet told me what had happened. Even before I saw you. There was too large a silence in my heart, and I couldn't breathe. I fell to my knees. If it hurt I didn't feel it. I just wanted to hold you. You were so still. Already cold. Your eyes wide open. I wanted to kiss you but didn't want to feel your skin cold under my lips. What if it made me forget all the kisses that had gone before? The warm ones and the sweet ones and the urgent ones? What if you no longer smelled like you? What if all that was left was the scent of your shampoo and your lotion but not that scent that made you *you*? I remembered your kiss from this morning, its edge of melancholy, how it lingered with me as I rushed out the door.

Breathing hurts. The air is too heavy for my lungs. I close your eyes and press you tight to me and time passes. I don't know how much time. I try to breathe and then I'm sobbing and sobbing and can't breathe for all the tears. You're gone. You're gone and I'm alone and not alone because you are still with me and I can still hold you.

You are safe here. In my arms. I won't let you go. I'm sorry I wasn't here. You needed me and I wasn't here. I wanted to always take care of you. Wanted to be your refuge and your home. Wanted my love to flood away all your past. Wanted to hold you until you never felt the need to flinch.

Your hair is as soft as it ever was. I smooth it away from your face. Kiss your eyelids. Nothing will ever hurt you again, *amapola mía*. No more pain. No one can ever hurt you again. No one will ever touch you again. I will make it so that my hands are the last hands to touch you.

I wipe away my tears. I need to carry you to the bedroom. I slide one arm under your back, another under your knees but can't lift you that way. I prop you up so that you are sitting up, leaning against the couch. Then I place my feet on each side of your hips, lock my hands behind your waist and pull up until you are on the couch. From here, I can pull you over one shoulder. I wish I could carry you any other way. You're not heavy, but you're taller than I am. I don't want your fingertips to drag along the floor but I'm afraid that's what they're doing. I carry you to the bedroom and lay you down. Slide the pillow beneath your head and cover you with the white lace coverlet you love. I stay there for a while, tracing the lines of your face. Touching your skin, still impossibly soft and bright, both gold and cinnamon. Time passes.

You're gone but I still turn off the ceiling fan so you won't get cold. I pull away the lace coverlet. Fold it. You only have a robe on, over a thin T-shirt and panties. I remove them as gently as possible and remember all the times I put you to bed after a little too much drinking. Sometimes you'd wake up giggling and pull me toward you. Sometimes you'd stir in your sleep and start screaming, start slapping and kicking me away.

I wait to see what you will do. But nothing. No invitation. No fight. Only stillness.

I brush your long hair first, brush it until it shines, until it radiates in every direction from your face. Dark waves. I've always loved your hair. It was what caught my attention first, the way it swayed against your back as you walked. How soft it was every time I dug my hands, my face, into it. How you'd lean forward sometimes so that your hair screened your face. How I loved it when you'd drag your hair over my body, its whispering softness on my breasts, on my thighs, on my back. When I first met you, I used to fantasize about wrapping it around my wrist, about pulling on it until your chin jerked up. Keeping you that way. But I taught myself to not want it. Brushing your hair, I am not tempted. Just the thought fills me with a soft horror.

I drag the large folding table out of the closet and set it up by the bed. Go to the second bedroom and collect my silk thread, my thinnest needles, my scissors, my soft blue pencils. From the linen closet in our bathroom, I bring out the little washcloths and the French lavender soaps you loved best. Your favorite towel, the one with the tree and its hundred differently colored leaves. I fill a basin with warm water.

I lather the long lines of you. Your arms, your wrists, your hands. Your small breasts, your long abdomen, your hips, your thighs. Your long, long legs. It seems so long ago, that first morning we lay naked, facing each other, silent, eyes wide, reaching out to softly touch. Withdraw. Touch again. So gently learning each other. Somehow making us more each other's more thoroughly than we had the night before. The silence ended when I touched your back and you giggled uncontrollably. Your always ticklish shoulder blades. Impossible now that you aren't flinching and pushing me away. Impossible that you're so silent. I turn you around and lather your back. With your body on the bed, it's nothing to move your limbs this way and that. Soap you rinse you dry you. Change the sheets beneath you. I say no goodbyes to your body—I will never say goodbye. I kiss your eyelids and cover you again.

It takes me two hours to gather everything. I pull out a small basket and shears from the hallway closet with your gardening supplies. I go out to the backyard and start clipping. I want to bring them all in—every rose, petunia, gardenia, sunflower, hibiscus, dianthus blossom. Every bougainvillea, jasmine, *esperanza*, hollyhock. There's no way to know how many I'll need, and you'd loved them all.

I choose only the most beautiful blossoms, without scars, just opened, the most fragrant. Only the most beautiful of each kind of flower. As I clip them, their aromas, sweet and sharp and subtle, commingle with the scent of their green limbs bleeding.

I see you in every flower, remembering you on hands and knees planting each one in the earth. When you were planting these poppies, I wiped dirt from your cheek before bending down to kiss it. To taste the salt of your sweat on your neck. You laughed and grabbed my shoulders and pinned me to the ground under you.

"I'm not one of your plants," I cried.

"Yes, you are," you said, tossing handfuls of loose earth on my chest.

"I'm going to plant you here and water you until you blossom."

I grabbed your hands. "I don't think I'd make very pretty flowers. You're the beautiful one."

You stopped, leaned in close and brushed the dirt off my face. "You're my earth. Without you there'd be no flowers. *Mi tierra*, that's what I'm going to call you forever." And you kissed me.

And I breathed, "*Amapola mía*." against your golden skin.

I see it as I'm choosing the brightest of the sunflowers. An hour until dusk. Still plenty of light. It's at the far end of the yard, between the shed and the fence. Head lowered. Hackles raised. *Coyotl*. That's what you'd always called it. Even motionless, it somehow looks broken. Not black but the color of mottled blood stained with fresh crimson. I could see the white bones of its legs exposed in places through the matted fur. I'd never known what to say when you'd tell me it was there. That it had come and gone many times in your life. That when it was there, you could see it out of the corner of your eye. When it was there, its howling kept you from sleeping at night. That you heard it even when you weren't at home. Even when you thought you were okay. Even when you were happy and in my arms.

It growls at me. I look at it head on. Its eyes are two bottomless holes that swallow all the light. I won't let it have you. It won't take you. I meet the absence of its eyes with all the anger and grief tossing inside me. It stays in its corner while I back away and enter the house through the patio door. I don't take my eyes off it as I close and lock the wrought-iron door and slide the patio door closed. For the tiniest fraction of a moment, I lower my eyes and assure myself that the basketful of flowers is undamaged. That's all it takes. The *coyotl* is a dark blur in the yard, and then its body is crashing against the iron bars. Again and again, all teeth and ravaged flesh. I hurry. The front door is locked tight. The door in the kitchen leading to the garage is the flimsiest door we have. I lock it, bolt it, push the heavy wooden dining table against it. I run from room to room, locking doors and windows. Drawing all the curtains. I don't want it looking in.

I can still hear it. It's throwing itself against the door. Sounds of wet flesh. I wonder if it will tear itself apart.

I rush back to you. Lay the basket on the table and take you into my arms. I put the *coyotl* out of my mind.

I only want to think of you as I do this, murmuring low, so low, against your skin. And even when I am quiet, every time I breathe, every time I exhale, you will know I am calling to you, *mi flor, mi cielo, mi reina, mi vidita*. I examine each petal, laying them softly against each other, spread in a magnificent spill of colors across your skin. Across your limbs. I hold them to your skin, wanting to find the colors, the petals that best follow each other. I will layer them so that my tiny stitches will be invisible.

When I was making your wedding dress, I breathed, "I will love you forever," into every single pierce and pull of the needle. I remember your voice, "Like fish scales!" you cried out, laughing and staring in fascination.

"Do you trust me to do this, love?" I asked when I was sewing together the three hundred diamond-shaped panels that formed the skirt of your wedding dress.

"Always! Even if you make me look like a fluffy mermaid!" you murmured against my neck and kissed me.

I love you now more than I did then. This time I will breathe love into each push of the needle and draw out your pain with each pull. All the pain I wasn't strong enough to hold for you.

I unspool the silk. Thread the needle. Your skin is silk. My sighs are silk. Silk my breath. Silk my eyes. Silk my hands. Purple petunia petals and white and pink rose petals on the soles of your feet, on your toes, around your ankles. How easily the needle moves in and out of your skin. Looping whispers. Sunflower petals, red and peach and yellow hibiscus, golden marigolds on your calves and knees and thighs.

I line up each petal, six stitches on the upper half of each side, enough to secure each petal, touching each one as little as possible with my hot hands. You always said my hands were like small suns, radiating heat. I could never believe how cold you always were to the touch. I always held your hands to keep them warm, tucking them against my throat or blowing my warm breath on your fingertips. You begged me often to rub your back and your feet. You're cold now, but my touch does nothing to warm you. You lay there, still and quiet. You used to slip your hands into my pockets and joke about putting a bun in my oven and then giggle at my grimace. You don't sigh as my hot hands move from your feet to your calves to your thighs. Your cold flesh doesn't respond to the hot tears falling on your skin.

How I love you. How I've always loved you. How many times did I hold your delicate jaw in my hands, studying your large eyes with their soft expression. I'll never understand how you could be so kind when you'd known so much hurt. How you could radiate light and tenderness when you were given so much darkness and brutality. I held you in my arms and wanted to kill them, wanted to set them ablaze and listen to the crackle of their flesh. It took all I had to be still, to listen, to know that holding you while you spoke was the most necessary thing I could do while you told me about the uncle who raped you on your tenth birthday. The college boyfriend and his friend who drugged you and raped you in your own bed. How no one believed you, and the college did nothing with your testimony. The unknown guy who attacked you in a parking lot the spring after you came out. He wanted your number and wouldn't take a no. When you told him you liked girls, he turned violent.

How you loved me. No one ever loved me the way you loved me. My life had gone by, one woman and then another. Never alone for any long stretch, but never with one for very long either. And when they said goodbye, we were done. "*Bruta*," they said as they left, "you don't know how to love anyone."

But with you I had no say. I didn't choose to let you in. Didn't choose to love you. One day I didn't even know you, and the next, you were my everything. And it poured out of me, all this tenderness I didn't know was inside me.

Sometimes at night I held you and wept. I couldn't take away your memories, the fear that woke you in the middle of the night, the anxieties that took over your days. No one knew what it cost you to live as you lived. Choosing every day to put away the past, choosing every time to help all the young women that came to you with their own nightmares and memories. No one knew how their stories made you rage and scream and left you gasping for air. When you wept in my arms your shoulders rocked so hard I feared you'd come apart. I left my tears for when you couldn't hear me, couldn't see me. So that you'd never know what it cost me to listen. And when you were awake I said, I love you, and I said, I love you, and I said I loved you a hundred times because I wanted you to believe it.

Midnight. The sound of wood bursting and cracking and splintering. I grab the machete I always keep by our bed. Run down the hall toward the kitchen. The *coyotl* making a sound I'd never heard a creature make before. Part growl, part bark, part howl. One reversed paw caught in the door between the garage and the kitchen. The hollows of its eyes seem more pronounced in the huge misshapen head. Its long-pointed ears swiveling, following my every movement. Its nostrils flare as I get closer. With every breath, it makes low whistling sounds like the scraping of rusted metal. Then it screams as it pulls its leg free. No time to think, I swing the machete. Spray of black blood on the wall, on the floor. It contorts in mid-air to avoid the blade, falling hard on its side. Its too-long legs scrabble wildly. It makes a horrible wrenching sound as it gets to its feet, spine rippling impossibly. There's a wrongness to it that makes me want to look away—sometimes moving like a coyote-like creature, sometimes like a spider, sometimes like a boneless thing, all rolling flesh and bloodied fur.

It growls at me. I stand my ground, both hands around the machete's handle. It shifts, from one side to the other at irregular intervals. I breathe, waiting, watching, ready. The rasping whistling sounds grow louder.

I snarl at it. Keep snarling. It starts in my chest, flooding into my throat, building in intensity until my whole body is thrumming with it. I let the growling free. A deep cold spirals through me, leaving me feeling stronger and lighter. My face changes. Lengthens. I reach to touch my cheek and find only bone. The flesh of my hands is falling away, bones of my fingers touching the bones of my face. But nothing hurts. There is no blood. Only the bones of me released, set free, exposed to the air. I fall to all fours. My shoulders wider, stronger. Spirals of bone within my ribcage. There is no flesh. I remember this lightness, this strength, this cold radiating from me.

The *coyotl* lowers its head, releases a garbled shriek, launches itself at me. The bare bones of my paws skitter loudly on the tile but I run toward it, both of us in mid-air when we ram into each other. We both land on all fours. I rear up and close my jaws around what should be its throat. Keep my jaws locked even as I feel its flesh rolling away from my grasp. As soon as it's free, it throws itself away from me, landing on its strangely reversed paws. I stay quiet, watching it, weight on my haunches, ready to lunge.

It takes a step backwards, still making rasping sounds. Another step, the hollows of its empty eyes growing larger and darker. It retreats step by step. The heat in my eyes builds and builds until it feels as if my head must burst into flame.

There's no way to contain it in the kitchen. No doors to close between where I stand and the bedroom door. The night is passing. You're still waiting for me.

I take a step back. It doesn't follow me. Another step. And then another. It watches me make my way down the hall. I open the door, step inside, move to close it. In the last second, I see it barreling toward me. Just enough time to brace my head and shoulders against the door before it comes crashing against it. The door barely makes a noise. I hear it move away. The whistling sounds disappear.

I stare at my hand. Concentrate. The bone elongates, the flesh returns. I lock the door. I'm standing upright by the time I reach the dresser. I push it against the door. I'm breathing too quickly. There's a slight quiver in my hands, in my gut. I steal a glance at the mirror. I'm me again. But at the same time, I'm not. There's too much light coming out of my eyes. My skin's slightly luminescent. Am I imagining everything? Am I going a little mad, here, with you, your body, with these flowers, only me, only me here with you?

I turn back to the bed. Keep my eyes lowered. Hoping, still hoping I'll hear your voice and you'll open your eyes and reach your hand out to me. I wait. Silence. Stillness.

Still so many flowers waiting. But this time I don't hesitate. The lavender peonies are next. Each flower so heavy in my hand. You laughed at me when I said they felt alive, alive like animals, trembling in my hands. I lay the petals on your thighs. My fingers are shaking. I force them still. I can't make mistakes. Won't mar your skin. One petal and then another. And me, remembering. My lips know—no, they *knew*—every bit of you, every dip and swell, every fold, every flutter and shudder. I knew the center of you, your taste and feel. Knew what made your body sing, what made it seize. Release.

You are gone. How much longer will I be able to remember you like this?

But I'll never forget your flinching. The nights you wept and shook in my arms. The nights you shrank away from me, unable to bear even my touch. I learned to never take my eyes off you. You were quick to return my kisses, easy with casual affection. I could hug you, hold you, kiss your neck, hold your hand, spoon you. But sometimes, as the intensity built and I longed to lose control, you'd become hesitant. And I learned to give you space without leaving you alone. Other times, we were able to drive out each other's memories until I was the only one who'd ever touched you and you were the only one who'd ever touched me.

Petal after petal, each one as soft as the flesh they cover. For your hips, blue hydrangeas, their multicolored petals like flickering butterflies against you. Deep blue irises on your belly, blue poppies over your hipbones. Do you remember? The day I surprised you with blue poppies? I came home early from a week-long trip, turning the key and putting my things down quietly, quietly. I found you lying on the bed on your stomach, your face buried in a book. I loved surprises but you hated them. Didn't stop me from wanting to see sudden delight on your face. I tiptoed to the bed and laid the flowers by your side. Waited. Minutes passed. You turned the page, reached for another pillow and felt the soft coolness of the blossoms against your arm. You smiled and turned to where I was.

"Baby!" I yelled and jumped on the bed.

You giggled as I climbed over you, kissing every bit of you I could reach. Your cheek, your shoulder, your elbow.

"You're home! You're home!"

You flipped me over and then moved away, pulling on my hands. "Up! Up!" Until we were both jumping up and down on the bed, laughing so hard there were tears in our eyes. We collapsed, side by side, still laughing. And I touched your face and you kissed my fingers.

No change in the darkness. What time is it. How many hours till morning. How many hours since I'd barricaded the door. How many hours of painstaking stitches.

I pause. Let my eyes close. Lay down the needle. Flex my hands. White magnolia petals for your upper abdomen, beneath your breasts. Your scars are vanishing. No one will ever see them again. Question them again. No more scars. No self-inflicted scars. No scars inflicted by others.

These flowers are your new skin.

"I was only fifteen the first time I tried," you told me. "My mother had promised me I'd spend the summer with her, but then her new boyfriend suggested they take a road trip, and I knew what that meant. I thought pills would be easiest. I skipped school and came home while she was at work. I should have had six hours to myself, but the neighbor saw me come home and called my mom at work. I tried again a year later when I found out I was pregnant. The third time was in college. I didn't want to live if my whole life was going to be one hurt after another. I thought my life had to be cursed. After the attack in the parking lot, I decided I'd hang on even if no one cared. It was ten years before I tried again. A year before I met you."

I remember the first time I feared you'd leave me. You were too quiet. You didn't want to get out of bed. Your mother had died. You found out by email. A cool, short message from a cousin. Fifteen years since you'd spoken to your mother—because of what happened when your uncle died. You'd told her the truth, but she couldn't hear it. Didn't want to hear it. Not her brother, she'd said. She made you leave the funeral. It was impossible to forgive her, you'd said, for not protecting you, for not believing you. Even dead, she took his side.

I didn't know what to do. Your silence after that email scared me. I didn't know if I needed to stay with you. If I needed to take days or weeks off work for you. If I needed to cook all of your meals and make sure you ate. I didn't know whether to hold you or leave you alone, make you talk or remain quiet. I called every day, on my breaks, during lunch and on my way home. I woke up every time you got up from our bed at night. Held you tighter. Grateful for every day I had you. While you slept, I kept guard over you, willing the nightmares to keep their distance, vigilant for the slightest frown on your face.

That was the first time. There were other times. I learned to push down my fear.

Morning is coming. It's been too many hours now. My fingers are stiff. The joints keep locking. A tiny electric pain is shooting from the palms of my hands to my wrists, but I can't stop. No stopping until I'm done. Soft pink petals on your breasts. Each petal so terribly still. No breath to flutter them, no warmth to make their scent exude, no beating heart beneath my hands. Only stillness. Only coolness.

I remember the heat of your mouth on my collar bone, the heat of you against my hand, how urgently you rocked your body against mine. I liked all the sounds you made against my throat, your arms wrapped around me, your hands pulling at my hair. I wanted that moment each time, to be looking into your eyes every time your body tightened around me. To catch that sigh of release with my mouth. To trace your cheek while

I memorized the soft dreaminess of your expression. The same way you looked the last time I found you in the garden … just after you'd planted the new flower plugs you'd brought from the store. So tiny, barely more than root and a stem and two leaves. Your hands were patting the soil around them when I knelt on the earth to kiss you, to catch that sigh of satisfaction with my mouth.

Silk thread rising. Needle piercing. Hardly any resistance. Silk thread running.

You unmake me. You uproot me. You scatter the earth I cling to. I don't belong anywhere, only here with you. I have never belonged anywhere before. Vine-colored magnolias for your shoulders. White jasmine petals for your throat. One deep red rose petal for the hollow of your throat.

Only your face is left now. I choose the last flowers. Place them on the pillow.

I can't begin. Though the petals are in my hand. Though I have needle and thread ready in the other. Though I know dawn is coming. I can't begin. I put everything down. Lie next to you—not close enough to crush any of the flower petals, only close enough that I can look at your profile the way I used to. While you slept next to me. I can pretend for a moment that I'm not saying goodbye to the curve of your cheek, the line of your lower lip, the arc of your brow. I can pretend that if I kiss the tip of your nose, you'll scrunch up your face and open your eyes and scowl at me for waking you. I can pretend your cheek is warm when I reach to touch it. Soon, neither I nor anyone else will ever see it again. I drag myself away from you, sink to my knees on the floor besides the bed.

It's so loud it feels like the door is bursting all around me. The wood shrieks. The dresser is flung on its side. The machete is out of reach, useless on the other side of the bed. The *coyotl* leaps toward you, its jaws opening, dripping saliva and blood.

No time to think or feel or scream. I throw myself at it and we collide. I'm not woman-shaped. I'm this new thing again, these spirals and links of white, white bone. I feel my shoulder ram its side. It rears its head and locks its jaws around the bone of my throat. But there is no flesh there, nothing susceptible to its teeth. No flesh to cringe away from its amorphous fur, rolling and heaving.

There's a roaring in my chest. I pull it closer to me, tightening my grasp until my long bone arms can reach all the way around it. I whisper against its head, "She's not yours. I am her heart. You are nothing."

I hold it. Tight and tight and tight. Stare into the abyss of its emptied eye sockets. I make no other sound. I peer into that emptiness until it gives way and I see a heaving ocean of blood. I dive in, moving through a world of red until I come to stand on a deserted beach. The moon is glimmering through rushing purple clouds. The *coyotl* is there, lying on its side, panting up at me. Its eyes are a flickering gold. It speaks and its voice comes from everywhere and nowhere.

"This is not how I began. This is not what I was. I was a *xoloitzcuintli* once, accompanying the souls of warriors to the other side. I never faltered. I knew my place in the turning of the earth and the sky and all life. I would go to them. They would rise and together we would walk, slipping from this world to the next. They were all warriors, even the ones who died by their own hand. The despairing dead. I found bodies pierced by unknown weapons. Bodies eaten by dogs. Fields of bodies decimated by disease. The tortured, maimed, raped, abandoned. I passed from this world to the other without stopping, day after day, moon after moon, year after year. It was my nature to love them. I could not be anything other than what I was. I loved them and they despaired. I licked their hands and drew as much pain from them as I could, so they could go, brave and bright, into the other world. I don't know when I started to change, when I became bloodied and misshapen."

Glimmering bones suddenly appear in the air above the *coyotl*. They solidify and fall, pinning the *coyotl* down. It whines, high and sharp.

"She said she saw you for fifteen years. Why terrorize her for fifteen years?"

"I came to her much earlier. The first time she tried to kill herself, I was there to take her to the other side. But she survived. That attempt and the next and the next. I knew she saw me. I know I am not a beautiful thing anymore. And I am not always sane. Five centuries and more of blood and pain live in my flesh. Five centuries and more of despair took my eyes. Took my voice. Took my reason. I forgot who I was, but I would not leave her. Because I must take her to the warriors. You love her. Help me do what I came to do."

On this strange beach, with its blood waves and its glimmering moon and its rasping wind, I kneel before the *coyotl*. The long shards of bone are burning away its flesh. I can see its heart. I plunge my hand deep, deep, until it is clenched around the beating thing. I stare into the heat of its eyes. "This is how much I loved her," I say and tighten my fist until I am screaming. And then it is screaming and howling and whistling all at once. And its flesh melts away, revealing the same white spirals of bone my face and arms and chest are made of. The stench disappears. The blood disappears. The wind moves through the whorls and hollows of its skull.

"Come with me," I say.

It nods.

I open my eyes. You're still on the bed, black hair radiating outwards. Your shining face still bare. I reach for the silk thread but it slips through my skeletal fingers. I stare at my hands, willing the flesh to return. I lay the last petals, red and white camellia japonica, across your chin, your right cheek, your nose, over your eyes and across your brow all the way to your hairline. An entire red passionflower rests on your left cheek.

I look up. The *coyotl*, now white and gleaming, a marvel of spiraling bones, nods, its golden eyes burning steadily.

I hold your flowered hand. We wait. The sun rises. The light travels across the room, from the gauzy bedroom curtains to the dresser. Slowly, the sun moves toward the bed. I watch as the light pauses before touching your body. An impossible breeze blows across the room, all the petals on your body fluttering.

You open your eyes. And you are you and there are no shadows in your eyes and there is no pain. You are here with me. You hold out a flowered hand and stroke my face. I take a hold of your hand and help you rise from the bed. The bone *coyotl* goes to you, and you rest your other flowered hand against its skull. There is nothing to say. Your flowered body ripples, and you make a sound like a dove cooing. You hold my hand to the flowers over your lips and then let me go. I watch the two of you move toward the sunlight streaming in through the window.

So much light.

marzipan

I dream you laid out before me. Flesh colored. Woman shaped. I bite into you, and you do not bleed. Candy sweet.

Your exact feet. Your precise toes. Your crimson nail polish. The small scar on your left ankle. Your strong calves. Your knees. I lean over you and catch the scent of almonds, honey, rosewater. I fill my mouth with your left thigh. There is no blood, only sweetness. I trace the lines of your hips. You look warm, look alive, but my hands touch coolness, touch the slight stickiness of sugary things. It had to have been a master artist to mold your rounded abdomen, the soft curves of you, the slight folds of you. These are your breasts, both upturned and not completely firm, obedient to gravity. A master artist to have painted your stretch marks and the blue pathways of veins. I look closer and see that your long hair is not hair but finely spun dark sugar. If I'm not careful, it'll break.

I hold you in my arms. My warmth warms you. The scent of you rises. What would it take to melt this candied you?

Your eyes are wide open.

I lick the rosy tint of your cheeks.

Will I tell you I dreamt of you this way? If I speak my secrets now, will you know them? If I hold your sugared body, does it make me less faithful to you? And what if your candied hands touched me with more tenderness? With a touch that was more eloquent than yours? What if your candied lips uttered what you never voice? And if I eat your sugared face, will you cease to be you?

What is it I want most? To take you within me or to erase myself? I think that if you dreamt of me this way, you wouldn't be as possessed as I am with this desire to devour.

I bury my face in the space between your neck and your shoulder and hear the crackling and snapping of your sugared hair.

huitzitzilin

"Don't speak to me," I say to them, my lips against their ears. "It's more than I can bear, to speak when I am naked and you are here, your words falling forever inside me.

"Kiss me, touch me, hold me," I say. "Bite me, taste me, pinch me, fuck me, but don't talk to me."

I am most myself in the dark, naked and not alone.

What I loved was the loss of gravity. And the hands that held me. Spun me. Caught me. The hands at my waist that pulled me, pushed me. Their bodies emanating heat. The brush of chest, breast, thigh. Hard arms holding me so close, so tight I thought my spine would leave an imprint on their chests. I loved the lights spinning dizzily, the rhythmic throbbing beat driving my body across the floor, the music bursting under my skin.

No more. The open space in my living room measures ten feet by twelve. I dance in silence, reconstructing forgotten songs, straining against myself. No spinning. No dangerous spill of intricate footwork. No sudden sharp turns of my hips. I'm constrained to slow circles, half-steps and lowered arms, dancing on my heels so as not to risk my balance. I can't afford to lose myself.

When I am alone, I am always a little lost. Inside, I am spinning, spinning. Unable to find North.

They came to sip at my eyes—a cacophonous cloud of iridescence. Bright bodies hurtling with stillness. Searing reds. Flashing blues. Black so black it reflected the light of dawn. So beautiful I wanted to touch them. Wanted to stand in the midst of all that humming, that spinning. Wanted to embrace their invisible limbs, the invisible air they made viscous, visible.

Waves of tiny shimmering bodies flung me to the ground. Covered me. I cried out and raised my arms. Too many. I beat them away but more came. The sound of all their vibrating bodies so loud against my skin. My bones shivered against my own flesh, blood trembling inside my veins. My heart seized. They held my eyes open. Their almost translucent tongues unfurled, laying grooved edges across the whites of my eyes. Piercing pain. Hot and jagged. But their wings were soft beating against my face.

Flickering colors and guttural sounds drinking deep, drawing the nectar out of my eyes, my body. Drinking my memories. My caresses. My soft dreams, my lost tears. Trickling moments of tenderness brought up from the soles of my feet, from the tips of my fingers. They drank deep. Drank the honeyed darkness coiled in the center of my heart. Everything sweet devoured.

I lay bleeding on the ground, watched the bright-winged creatures flicker away through a descending darkness.

It was morning. I'd gone to the park to watch the sun rise. I never saw it set.

I can't describe how the night is different. The absence of the weight of daylight on my skin. In the night, we shed our clothing, our daylight selves. Shedding blindness, shedding helplessness. I shed the woman who risks her life crossing the street, the woman who counts her steps, the woman who is always afraid.

I know the night. Light and shadow entwined. What it hides. What it reveals. The yearning that lives that burns that builds just underneath the skin. That drives us toward each other, collapsing the infinite spaces between strangers. I know the language of flesh, the first words spoken over skin, the sigh as mouth meets mouth as limbs entwine as flesh sinks into flesh. The gasps of arching backs. Touch translating need.

This is when I think the hummingbirds have nested inside me. Their quick breaths my harsh panting. The tintinnabulation of their tiny hearts thundering deep inside me. Their heat flashing through me. I sip the shadows from their necks. Musk on the tip of my tongue. Their scent and mine rolling over my skin. The slapping and pounding of flesh against flesh. Even in the dark there is the pulsing of tiny flickering flares. Curls of heat licking at my spine. Sweetness in them all. I drink and drink. Left breathless and spent.

"I love you, Xóchitl, let me take care of you. Come live with me, or I can live here with you."

"Not this again, Jorge. You take care of me enough."

"All I do is put money in your account. I want to be here to cook for you and drive you and be with you. Just you and me."

"*Ay*, Jorge, I would drive you crazy in a week. You need someone who needs you all the time. I like being alone most of the time. I like doing things for myself."

"But I want to do those things for you …."

"Which is why we'd never work. Whatever happened with that daughter of your mother's cousin's coworker's friend?"

"My mother's neighbor's daughter? That's why I haven't gone to go see my mother. I think they're trying to ambush me."

"*Ay*, don't be like that. Go meet the girl. You're the kind of man that needs a home and a wife and some little babies. I'm not that woman, so get that out of your head. What I'm good at is this . . . ."

"Xóchitl!"

"Shut up already. Come here."

I live alone. A small apartment. They tell me its walls are white and its ceilings vaulted. Six hundred and twenty square feet. My bed is in the exact center of my bedroom. I dislike stretching my legs or my arms and hitting a wall. One small nightstand to my left. One chair by the window. I like to sit there and feel the breeze. Six steps exactly to the door from the foot of the bed. Bathroom to my left. Washer and dryer in a closet to my right. Eight steps to an L-shaped combination of dining and living room. Clockwise: A stone mosaic table for two. Two director's chairs, one on each side. A sofa large enough to stretch out in. A ceramic statue of a woman bearing a water jug on her back. The ceramic feels porous and cool but alive under my fingers. Two blooming jasmines by the windows. The door. A narrow mahogany table. A plush rocker recliner. An expanse of wall. Kitchen to my left.

There are no knickknacks anywhere. No heap of old newspapers. No coffee table and no cozy lamp-lit corners. No books and no television. The walls would be bare, but I couldn't bear the thought of such a pale, pale living space. My sister brought paintings. Abstract whirlwinds of vivid colors, she said. I often feel the raised slaps, whirls, and dashes of paint with my fingers. When everything is still and quiet, it seems to me the walls grow warm. That the paint begins to move. Kaleidoscopic colors escape the canvases, streaming from one wall to the next, one room to another. Not the sound of water running. A thicker, deeper sound.

Such heat in his lips, such tenderness in his touch. I imagine his eyes are often shot through with light. Under my fingers, his hair feels golden. I trace his features over and over as if by dint of sheer repetition his face will come alive in my mind. As if I could make myself remember what I have never seen.

Jorge loves to be straddled. Loves to hold my breasts in his hands as I move. Loves to lie on his stomach and have me massage him while straddling his thighs. I measure myself against him. He is only slightly taller. I stretch myself against his back. His fingers barely reach further than mine. Powerful shoulders and arms and a rippling back. How I love to smooth my fingers against the small of his back, the firmness of his buttocks, down to powerful thighs and calves, his small broad feet. Everywhere a light dusting of curls for my fingers, for my lips. He makes sounds like a tamed wild cat, purring and growling, hissing. He loves to lay his head on my lap, loves to have me brush my fingers through his golden curls.

Ramón is nothing like Jorge. Long and lean, his limbs are an eternity to my hands. Wiry muscles taut over his bones. Elegant narrow feet and hands. His face seems sad to my hands. Deep eyes. They have to be dark. Have to be shadowed. He loves to hold me beneath him. Loves to stretch my limbs until the muscles protest. Loves sex against walls and on tables. Loves to wrap himself in my long hair. Loves that I don't love him, don't need him beyond this darkness. Loves knowing that if he never returned, I'd never pine after him. That if he said goodbye, I'd never set my body against his like an anchor, crying out his name as he walked away. And yet he loves that I never turn him away.

One is day. One is night. One is earth and one is sky. I taste one and sip the other. Drink one and devour the other.

And then there is Mercedes. Only Mercedes is allowed to spend the night, to bathe with me, to cook in my kitchen. I don't know what she tells her husband or her children when she is with me. I don't ask. I long to bite at her throat, to leave purple marks on her soft thighs, but I restrain myself. She trusts me, and she isn't mine. She holds her fingers to my lips when her cell phone rings. Her body goes from hot and pliable to cold and rigid as she turns away from me. A voice I don't recognize emerges from her.

After she hangs up the phone, I take her feet in my hands, warm them, running my fingers along the instep. Press my palms hard against the arch of her feet. Slowly, she melts, returns to me. I neither drink nor devour her. I breathe her. I inhale and exhale Mercedes.

I can't forget their wings. How did they mistake my eyes for blossoms? Violet sabrewings. Lucifer hummingbirds. Broad-billed hummingbirds. I saw them once, long ago, visiting a friend who lived just south of Tucson. What were they doing here, a thousand miles away from their path of migration?

Sometimes, lying in the dark, I think I can hear them. Even inside my bedroom with its closed windows. I make myself take deep breaths. Make myself sit up slowly. Move my head slowly from side to side, trying to pin down the tiny sound of humming wings. I reach out in slow arcs, methodically tracing the air around me. Something swoops by my ear, hits my left hand. I recoil. Where is it? I rise to my feet, wildly flailing my arms around. The sound grows louder. Louder in every direction. I feel wings brush against my cheek and cover my eyes with my hands. Stumble around the corner of the bed. Fall to my knees and bury my face against the mattress. Buzzing sounds against my back. They fly into my hair looking for my eyes. "You cannot have them," I say. "You cannot have anything else of mine."

"No medical reason." In other days, I would have beat my head against the wall until the light pierced my eyes. Five years since that morning and the specialists still can't tell me why I'm blind. "Everything is as it should be," they said. They sent me to a psychologist. What was there to say? I could never tell anyone about the hummingbirds. They would think I was crazy.

I only told my sister. Even she said it made no sense. Hummingbirds are the spirits of warriors who fell in battle, the spirits of women who died in childbirth. Servants of Huitzilopochtli, the god of war. I don't know why they would seek me out. I am no warrior. The only thing I have ever fought is this darkness. And solitude.

"Ramón, wake up. You're having a nightmare. Ramón."

"Lorena? Lorena?"

"No, Ramón, it's Xóchitl. You fell asleep. Ramón, you're hurting my arm."

"*Ay*, I'm sorry, Xóchitl. I thought you were … I'm sorry, I didn't mean to hurt you …."

"It's okay. I'm okay. You were shouting in your sleep. Here, drink some water."

"What was I saying?"

"You kept saying the same thing, over and over, but you were getting louder."

"What was I saying?"

"No, Lorena, no. Over and over again."

"I'm so sorry I woke you, Xóchitl."

"Don't be. I wasn't sleeping. I was waiting for you to wake up for round two."

After the hummingbirds, I cut my long hair. Tossed my lipsticks and nail polishes and makeup, my heels and my purses and most of my clothes. Abandoned my books, my photo albums, the hundred mementos of my life. Refused to see old friends after the first few awkward visits. I gave up my apartment and went to live with my sister for two years. Months spent lying sleeplessly in bed. Spent cursing my life, my eyes. She bought me simple clothing. Drawstring black pants to wear and solid colored T-shirts she embroidered so that I could tell them apart. It hardly mattered. Like a wooden doll, I sat for hours. Remembering and refusing to remember. None of my memories belonged to who I had become. Even my name was no longer mine. I forgot how the world was tied together. How things in the world stood apart from each other.

I was afraid I'd forget what colors meant. I made a map for myself. My mother's casket—white. My hair—black. The fringed leaves of the mesquite—green. The dress my mother made for me when I was seven—yellow. The color of the sky the day I slept by the lake's edge—blue. The night sky at the southern horizon—purple. Blood—red. I found memories for fifty other colors. I clenched my fists, holding the memory of colors so close, they seeped through my fingers. Reduced to flashes, reduced to whirs, reduced to whimpers.

I have memories of photographs. I trace and retrace my features trying to remember what I look like. Am I different now? Time runs, runs through itself, runs through me. The minutes would last an eternity if there wasn't breathing to tend to, heartbeats to count, my eyes that still require blinking. Outside, I am too occupied negotiating through a large unknown. Inside the unknown unfolds. Extends. Deepens. When I'm alone, the unknown closes in around me, presses down on me, steals my breath. I forget where the doors are and stumble against furniture legs, misjudge the width of doors, have to force myself to stop, breathe, begin again.

Do they know? Sometimes in the night, when one of them lies beside me, I want to cling to them, want to press my lips against their shoulders, want to weep and say, "don't go." Want to say, "don't leave me alone. Hold me, I want to say. Keep me from falling apart. Give the darkness shape. Texture. Make a path for me through the days."

But I stay silent. That is not what I am for. Not what they are for.

There are others. Sweet Xian with her exquisite mouth, who gasps tiny gasps when she comes. Roel, who says I remind him of his wife. She is a thousand miles away. He comes to me when he misses her past bearing. I let him call me by her name. Jeremy who is the only one who cannot pronounce my name. "So-shee," he says. I do not hold it against him. He is so young, I still smell the milk of his skin.

I don't want to need anyone. So I stay silent. I press myself against Jorge's side, grab the curls above his neck and nip his earlobes. I rake my nails down Ramón's back and offer him my neck when he lunges after me. I reach with my hungry hands, my hungry limbs for Mercedes. Taste and taste and taste Xian and Roel and Jeremy. I will make heat of it all. My loneliness made into lust. My not knowing. My fear. My long hours. With them and in the dark I am still beautiful. Their hands make me real. Their mouths make me solid. And so we begin again and again until it is ended and I can close my eyes and the darkness is absolute and I can sleep.

"You won't ever ask me to leave them—to leave him—will you?"

"No, Mercedes, no. I'm here whenever you need me. And when you don't, you don't even have to think about me."

"But I'm always thinking about you. I'm always counting down the days and the hours. I pick up and put down the phone half a dozen times every day because I want to hear your voice, because I want to make you laugh. Do you know where I tell him I go?"

"Where?"

"I tell him I need time to write. That I'm working on a novel. That I need time away from him and the boys to concentrate. I used to write a long time ago, when we met in college."

"What do you do when he asks to see what you're writing?"

"I tell him, no, that I'll show him when I'm done. But just in case, I meet up with this young woman in her twenties, a single mother working two jobs and writing a novel. I pay her for her drafts and then I take them home and file them carefully away. In case I ever need them."

"Smart. A paper trail."

"It's how I get this time with you. Though every other weekend isn't enough. But I can't do this more often."

"Well, then, we better make this time count. No more talking."

That night, I dreamt them all. Ramón, Jorge, Mercedes, Xian, Roel, Jeremy. I could see them, in a circle around me, and I was spinning and spinning, facing one and then another. Their faces lit, as if they were looking at a sun whose brightness I couldn't see, a sun whose warmth I couldn't feel. And there was a humming everywhere around us that made my bones vibrate inside my flesh. I wanted to get away from it. And then I realized it was coming from inside me. I was spinning and spinning, all their faces blurring. But even in the dream, I knew it wasn't about stopping and choosing one of them. I was the needle of the compass, spinning and spinning, because I couldn't feel *North*.

Without North, there was no East, no West, no South.

They were waiting for me to give them direction.

My sister believed it was a matter of finding the right doctor, taking the right test. But the months went by. I had to learn how to walk, how to count my steps, how to eat, how to listen, how to read, how to use a cane, how to negotiate my way through the darkness. But finally, I had to leave and make a life to replace the one that was gone. My sister couldn't understand. I was dissolving. The contours of my body fading into the shadows. Hardly hungry. Hardly feeling. A lost thing that was not a woman. I lost weight until all my bones protruded. Callouses on my feet. My dry skin peeling and cracking. My eyes always swollen from tears. No job. No friends. Unable to dance and no longer beautiful. I left to save what was left of myself.

I chose this city because I'd never lived here. Because though I'd never see it, this city had a wide river and trees everywhere. Because it was a real city with buses and sidewalks where I didn't have to be driven everywhere. I learned this city with the end of my cane.

I threw away my T-shirts and drawstring pants. Grew my hair long again, black and water straight. Brushing it is only a matter of time and attention, taking it in sections. I can't wear very much makeup, but I can wear some, using my fingers as my guide. Light colors on my lips, dark shadows on my eyelids. Moisturizers. No way to know if there are circles under my eyes. I bought my clothes by feel. How my body felt moving inside them. Trusted salesgirls to choose the colors. Chose which salesgirls to listen to by feeling out the timbre of their voices.

I didn't know what I was looking for. But I found it in this city. I learned my little neighborhood—how many steps, street crossings and curbs there were from my apartment to the grocery store, the bank, the post office, the coffee shop. Ramón I met soon after I arrived. Jorge a few months later. Mercedes a year ago. The others in the last six months.

I haven't lost any. They've stayed. They give my days shape. Dinner. Light conversation. Massages. Sex. "We pass the time enjoyably," I tell my sister. She doesn't understand and calls me a whore. I tell her I don't charge them. Some of them choose to put money in my account. Ramón sends his housekeeper to me twice a week to clean my apartment and stock my kitchen. Jorge pays the rent, brings me lingerie. Mercedes pays for the manicures and pedicures and my visits to her day spa. Jeremy always brings wine and flowers. Xian and Roel surprise me with unexpected gifts. They all know about each other. They all know to call before any surprise visits. Mostly, they all have their regular days, their regular nights.

Another dream. A field of flowers, blooms of every shape and hue. Such vivid colors, I felt as if I could taste them on the tip of my tongue. Trees with more blossoms than leaves, vines that twisted in ecstasies of color, the green earth swathed with streaks of red and yellow and white. I dreamt the sun was shining warmly on my body, my body naked and feathered and afloat on the breeze.

Sweetness. The perfume-drenched air made me dizzy. Morning glories. I couldn't resist the morning glories tumbling across the white fence. Summer sky blue with butter yellow centers. So sweet. My tongue unfurled, and I sipped. It spilled into me, light refracting inside me, tumbling and tumbling.

They won't stop talking now. They talk late into the night, talking and talking unless their mouths are otherwise occupied.

Ramón: "Lorena was so beautiful. She loved to travel. We lost count of how many trips we made before she got sick. The last trip was to Paris. She wanted to visit all her favorite places again, but she grew too weak, and we came back to the US in a panic."

Jorge: "My mom keeps asking me if I've kissed her neighbor's daughter yet. I keep telling her it's none of her business. Yesterday, she bought a four-foot teddy bear and told me that she and my dad will pitch in with the down payment for a house if I make them grandparents in the next two years. I told them, making grandchildren was no problem, it was finding a wife that was going to take a little more work."

Mercedes: "Can I show you these photos? These are my two babies at Little League. Here's Brian's 6th birthday party. Michael when he was born. These are from last summer when we went camping. This my husband. Yes, the boys look just like him."

Xian: "My parents won't have anything to do with me since I came out to them. My brother's trying to talk to them, but they're not having it. The last time I saw my mother, she was weeping and saying this never would have happened if we'd stayed in China."

Roel: "*A veces temo que ella se vaya a encontrar a otro. Hace dos años que no nos vemos. Muy peligroso regresar. Ojalá y tendré lo suficiente pa' traerla el siguiente año.*"

Jeremy: "I was eight years old the first time I kissed a girl. Her name was Melissa—all freckles and red hair. We were on the playground by the swings. She burst out crying and ran away right after."

They make me laugh, and they make me cry. I try to quiet them. But their words are always spilling out, even when they're not there. The more I listen, the more a space inside me opens up.

I woke tasting sweetness in my mouth.

Jorge was there. Beside me. In sleep, he'd flung his leg over me. I wanted to reach for his arm and shake him awake. But I didn't.

They had been here. In this room. I'd heard them in my sleep. Heard them under the bed. I raised myself up on one elbow. In the dark night, I waited, perfectly still and perfectly silent. They would betray themselves. I strained for the sound of their humming wings. Nothing. Only my own breath, too loud in the ringing silence. And the sounds Jorge made. Not snoring, only a heavy inhale, exhale, inhale. I settled back into bed. He murmured my name and nuzzled my shoulder. Warm breath over my skin. I couldn't help it, I turned toward him and wrapped my arm around him. He stirred awake. Through the long night, we moved together. I sipped at him, filling myself with his scent, the realness of him, his weight on me. The scent of him, sweet, not sweet, the scent stirring my memory. Pink and purple blossoms. My lips sought out the center of him.

The next night I lay in my bed alone, waiting for a knock at the door. Instead, I heard humming sounds that grew louder and louder, felt wings brush against my hair. I burrowed into my bed and covered my head with the blanket. I couldn't breathe. All their tiny bodies with their wings beating against me. I fought my way out of bed and ran to the living room. The swarm enfolded me.

I couldn't breathe. I couldn't breathe. I felt their tongues unfurling. The sensation of tiny feathery knives against the underside of my skin, a sharpness so thin my flesh didn't realize it should have begun to bleed. And I felt them drawing something from me, sweet and dark and swirling.

Humming. Everywhere, humming. Tiny wings fluttering against my legs, my arms, my hair. Grooved tongues on my thighs, my back, my neck. Sipping at me. My body wasn't mine anymore. It shuddered. It convulsed, their vibrations like an electric current.

I felt them on my face, my eyes. Heat spilled from my eyes and scratched at the darkness. Deep crimson swelled along the line of my throat. A bright lime green spilled down my shoulders, silver arcs pooling in my palms. Glossy black in swaths over my breasts, my ribs, across my hips, brightening into sapphire and violet down my thighs and calves. Black feet. Black hands. Wings both delicate and merciless unmaking me.

The light flooded in stronger and faster until all I could see was my luminescent flesh. Not fading. Not lost. Not dissolving. Tiny feathers like scales made of light burst from my skin. Spinning. Spinning. Liquid colors. Spinning. Spinning. Where is *North*? Is this what the god wants with me. He gave them direction. Told them to find the island in the middle of the lake. The island where they would see an eagle holding a snake, perched on a flowering *nopal*. Did we forget that he was also the god of direction.

I breathed. Where is *North*? Breathed. The wings went silent. I listened to an eternity between a beat of my heart and the next. Breathed. This way. I felt *North* in my blood, in my marrow, in my flesh.

He needed new servants. Not warriors but compasses for the lost. And if I was a compass, I would never be alone in the dark. I would always have *North*. I would always have the hummingbirds. I would always have the lost. And the sweet.

Knocking at the door. Mercedes calling my name. I rose from the floor, fumbled at the locks, opened it. Fell into her arms.

"What's wrong," she asked. "Are you okay, are you hurt?"

I couldn't speak yet.

She led me to the couch, wrapped her arms and legs around me. I rested. She held me, rocked me to sleep, singing a lilting melody, her lips against my neck. I slept deeply. Woke in the darkest part of the night. She was spooning me. I twisted out of her arms. Slipped my hands under her shoulders. Shook her just enough to wake her.

"Xóchitl?"

I didn't let her say anything else, my lips hard against hers.

I felt her heart pounding suddenly against me. She didn't hesitate, letting me into her mouth, drawing her knees up around me. Red flowers, I saw red flowers in my mind when I kissed her, long and slender crimson petals. So much sweetness. Her hands in my hair, pulling it back when she moved her lips across my jaw, when she bit my earlobe. No words, only the sounds of mouths and flesh and grunting. We collapsed together, sweat-slick and gasping for air. Sleep.

And then dawn. More light than I'd seen in five years. I could almost see her. I leaned in close, trying to see the curve of her cheek, the brightness of her eyes, the line of her brow. I didn't want to blink, wanted to let all the light inside me. All the colors swirled into each other. No depth perception. I had to close my eyes to follow her into the shower, to get dressed, to sit at the table and have juice and toast with her, to walk her to the door and kiss her again and again. She didn't want to leave.

"It's all right," I told her, "I will always be here."

I had to close my eyes so I could breathe in the warm scent of her. Sunlight and wild grass.

I climbed my furniture and lay my face against the paintings. The colors ran under and over each other. Red. Purple. Yellow. I opened the windows and leaned out. Blue sky. Leafy trees. Green. I ran to the bathroom, fumbled for the light switch. Leaned in close to the mirror. Olive skin. Dark shadows where my eyes should be. Darkness around my face. My hair. Black.

I dove into my bed, almost dizzy. Stretched from the tips of my toes to the tips of my fingers, closed my eyes and watched colors move behind my eyelids. Dizzy and happy. I could feel *North*. I moved my arms and felt the humming around me respond. I wasn't alone. When night came, I went to stand by the window and watch the stars go in and out of focus. The light advanced and receded.

I was at the window when I saw Ramón on the sidewalk, headed toward my door. It was Ramón, there was no mistaking his long limbs or the hunching of his narrow shoulders. He'd brought wine. We sipped it in front of the fire he built, stretched out on the carpet. I'd thought the flames would have kept my attention but couldn't keep my eyes from his face. Such deep grooves around his mouth. Lines on his forehead and arcing from his eyes. His hair was too long. He kept brushing it away from his forehead. I reached up to hold his hair back. I wanted to see the flames reflected in his eyes, but it was as if purple clouds were floating in mine. A glimpse of gold, a glimpse of darkness and then the purple would obscure my vision. I lifted my head to lay tiny kisses along his jawline.

He flinched away from me. "What are you doing?" I had never done it before. Never held him with tenderness and softness. Never laid my hands against his face or smoothed his hair away. I'd never leaned in close toward him and laid tiny kisses along his jaw. He closed his eyes and stayed still, terribly still, against me. I unbuttoned his shirt, moved my hands gently across his chest, then my lips.

"It is all right," I whispered over his heart. "It's all right for us to be gentle with each other. It doesn't change your love for her."

His touch was like smoke. The scent of *cenizo* within his skin. The bloom and the leaves and even its scent after it's dried. Smoke and sage in his mouth. And though he left before dawn, the night was soft and long.

I kept waking up afterwards, feeling the softness unfurl inside me.

Humming all around me. How different it sounded now. Soft, like water. I held out my arms and they looped and swirled around them. They followed me everywhere I went. I held up my black hands, my olive-skinned hands, where I could see them. The same and not. But I recognized them both. These doubled hands were the hands I'd used to make my lovers writhe. This doubled body the one I'd made into a shadow flitting above them, sipping at them, filling myself with their sweetness. Ramón. Mercedes. Jorge. I speak their names and they are sweet on the tongue. Xian. Jeremy. Roel. I don't feel desperation for them anymore. When I move, I can't feel shards of glass grinding against each other—only humming and the sounds flowers make when their blossoms open.

The light comes and goes. The darkness comes and goes. When it is night and I am alone, I reach for no one. That is not what I am for. I am here until Jorge admits he has fallen in love with his mother's neighbor's daughter. Until Ramón lets himself love someone again. For as long as Mercedes needs me. Until Roel is reunited with his wife. Until Xian finds a love she can make a family with. For Jeremy for as long as he wants me. And there will be others whose scent will draw me. I am not refuge. I am not a crossroads. I am not *North* but I know where it lies. That is what I am for.

My tongue unfurled. My arms unfurled. My flesh unfurled. I am flower and nectar and hummingbird all at once.

I live in the same apartment, in the same city. No longer afraid. There is darkness and light and color and heat and sweetness and both solitude and company in the night.

The hummingbirds are always with me now.

Everything is nectar.

los ocelotes del norte

All we ever wanted to do was make music. And nothing, not even death, could stop us. We all went at the same time, me and Guale and Riche and Chino and Tim. It was one of those things—an eighteen-wheeler, heavy rain, a stubborn driver who shoulda admitted that that 2 a.m. Whataburger coffee wasn't working for shit.

All together, we left behind three ex-wives, two wives, two girlfriends, three boyfriends, nine children and six grandkids. We went to our own funeral—they did the *rosarios* and the burials at the same time. I didn't really want to see what was left of me lowered into the ground but it seemed disrespectful to skip out on it when everybody showed up and cried and told stories and ate and played our music. Our mothers, fathers, siblings, cousins all came. A lot of musicians and their families. And more fans than I would have imagined. They ran out of food at the reception after the funeral. A couple hundred people ended up putting together a barbecue on the spot, and the music played till night came and on and on until dawn. And people danced and sang and cried. I couldn't have asked for a better goodbye.

It wasn't so much a surprise to wake up after we died as it was to realize that the next world was the same world. Same everything. Same people. Same sun. Same earth. Only we were different, not see-through ghosts, not fleshy bodies, not on our way to following any kind of tunnel of light. We were still us, but we were *calaveras*, nothing but bones and the light inside.

It turned out the next world was also known as the Small World. Alive, I'd been 5'10". Dead, I was maybe 8 inches tall.

In my first memory, we're at the flea market and my mother is telling me and my little sister Lita that we can choose one toy. Just one. I knew which one I wanted. Couldn't see anything but that shiny red toy accordion. It was heavier than it looked. My arms were barely long enough to hold it when it was fully extended.

"This is your Crismas, Joaquín," my father grunted at me.

I nodded eagerly. It was okay. I didn't want or need anything else. Later, when I turned eight, my godparents bought me a real kid's accordion. I saved my weekly dollar allowance for years. Worked with my dad and worked side jobs and saved every penny until I was able to buy my first Gabbanelli. It was used and a little beat up, okay, a lot beat up, but it was a Gabbanelli—like I used to see Sunday mornings on "The Johnny Canales Show" when we lived in the Valley. *Barbacoa*, *pico de gallo*, scrambled eggs and beans for breakfast, and then we'd all sit to watch Johnny and all the bands.

I liked the Tejano bands—Selena and La Mafia and Mazz—and there was Rubén Ramos and Fito Olivares and Bronco, but it was the *conjuntos* that made the blood fire up in my veins. Ramón Ayala y Los Bravos del Norte, Los Huracanes del Norte, Los Cadetes de Linares and most, most, most of all, Los Tigres del Norte. I bought all their cassettes and listened to them over and over again. When I was at school, all I had to do was close my eyes and I could hear the lyrics, my toe tapping to the oomp oomp oomp, my shoulders trying to resist the little back and forth and my fingers spasming when it was time for the trill of the accordion. The sound of it shot straight through my soul. I thought if the heart could make music, it would sound like an accordion.

I was twelve when the movie *La Bamba* came out. I wanted to be like Ritchie Valens carrying his guitar around everywhere he went. But an accordion is more bulky than a guitar, and I got sent home from school, even though I told them I just wanted to be like Ritchie. Make my music, find my Donna, go out in a blaze of glory.

When I died, I thought I was going to see Amá and Apá and my brother Carlos. But nothing. I didn't know anyone ... except for Guale and Riche and Chino and Tim. It took a while to figure out that there were multiple worlds for the dead. It must be that the Creator knows your soul and sends you where you're supposed to go.

It took a while to figure out how things were different in the Small World and to adjust to the strangeness of bodies that weren't flesh and blood. We could taste and feel and lust and hurt, but all those things were somehow sharper, born and burning in our very souls.

No one asked us to choose. It was just given to us: the freedom to do what we'd wanted to do all our lives. Make music.

That was what people did in the Small World—what they most wanted to do. Painters painted on canvases small and immense, between walls and underneath houses, adding beauty in ways that the Big World would never see. There were tiny cafes with the most perfect desserts and immense feasts presided over by passionate chefs. All our gardeners were master gardeners, curating fields of wildflowers and tiny elaborate bursts of beauty. The woodcarvers carved, the weavers wove, the poets daydreamed and stared at the sky and then read their poems on street corners and on stages. The singers sang every kind of music. And the dancers danced—all bones and passion and light. In the Small World, we made our art without the Big World concerns of paying rent or making money. Without worrying about what our families thought. Without ambition or competition or envy or worries over whether or not we were successful. We lived in death what we had always known in life, that there was no greater purpose for our existence. All of us loved what we loved and were finally free to do nothing but what we loved.

At first I wondered why the Small World wasn't a separate world. Why keep us in the crevices and hidden places of the Big World? Why keep us where we could watch our loved ones? Why keep us in the world with its pain and suffering and asshole presidents and borders and pollution? Why keep us in the world?

There was an early morning. Breakfast tacos and hot coffee at a roadside taco shack with the guys. Even without bodies, we stamped our feet from the cold and watched our breaths rise hot and smoky. Christmas wasn't too far off and the conversation turned to the gifts we would have bought our live ones. I was the only one without kids of my own, but I would have taken gifts to my stepkids and their kids. For my nieces and nephews. We wondered if they were planning to stay home and not take any chances. It had been almost a year since we died. Early February before the pandemic. Had we already lost family without knowing it?

We ended up sketching out a map so that we could check on all of them. All our people.

I thought, this is why the Small World could never be separate from the Big World. What art would we make if we lived in perfect comfort and bliss? What music would we make if there wasn't a need for consolation, a need to celebrate, a need to weep, a need to dance, a need to make beauty to combat all the ugliness of the world?

I found Guale and Riche and Chino when we were living in Hereford. My parents were farmworkers when they got married. By the time me and Lita came along, my dad had a truck and followed the harvest seasons from Edinburg in the Valley to Bay City to Oklahoma to Hereford and back to *El Valle*. I met Guale and Riche the first year we worked in Hereford, when I was in the third grade. Guale's dad owned Sánchez Body & Auto, and Riche's family owned the only Mexican *panadería* in town. They had the best pink cake in the world. We stopped by there every Sunday after church.

We met Chino in high school. His father had just died and his mom moved back to be close to her family. He was the most Asian-looking Mexican we'd ever seen, so Chino stuck as his nickname right away. Guale came out to us sophomore year. Even though it was already the nineties, rural Texas with a bunch of white farmer kids and Catholic Mexicans and Tejanos wasn't the easiest place to be yourself. Guale had been afraid we'd turn on him, but Riche and I just shrugged at him and said, "Wasn't like we didn't know, man, you making calf eyes at Alejandro Covarrubias every day in Biology." There were a few rough spots through the years, with his dad, with some of the other bands we shared a stage with, with random Mexicanos and Tejanos who objected to him having an arm around his latest boyfriend. But he always had all of us as backup. When his dad threw him out, he came to live with me and became my brother.

As for Riche, we used to mess with him all the time and tell him the girls couldn't stay away from him because he smelled like *pan dulce* and pink cake and donuts. He'd gotten two girls pregnant by the time he graduated high school, and his mom would chase girls away from the bakery with a broom. Chino's story was super simple. He loved the drums. He and Aracely met when they were twelve and they never loved anyone else.

I went to college in Lubbock after high school, thinking I'd become a history teacher or something and have the summers off to play music. I met Tim there in my Mexican-American history class. Tim was the most Mexican-looking Tim Sullivan I'd ever seen. In one short semester, I saw him go from Mr. Clean Cut ROTC American flag lover to Super Chicano Man. He grew out his hair and his beard. Wore nothing but T-shirts with slogans like "We Didn't Cross the Border, the Border Crossed Us" and "Sí Se Puede" or indigenous-looking shirts. He went from listening to George Strait and Hank Williams Jr. to taking up Tejano music and approving of my love for Los Tigres del Norte. "That's the music of the people, man," he told me.

What was most surprising was his voice. He only spoke Spanish with his mom, but that voice was something else. With *conjunto* music, the beauty and power of a voice isn't the first thing you listen for. Sometimes the voices are nasal or uneven or raspy or a little too weak, but that's all right if you have *it*. If your voice sounds like your heart got broken and it stayed in your chest that way, jagged and bleeding. If your voice sounds like you speak through broken glass, like you know loneliness and hurt and your sadness burrows all the way down, so far down you wouldn't think a human body could hold it.

So when Tim came along, that's when we really became Los Ocelotes del Norte.

We went on tour pretty much the way we'd done in the Big World. Stayed mostly in Texas, since the same distances seemed much longer. Had a regular circuit of Small World cities to visit along the border from El Valle to El Paso, from San Antonio to Austin to Houston to Fort Worth and always back up to Lubbock.

People fell in love and out of love, celebrated weddings and anniversaries. We played big concerts, small bars, music festivals. You haven't seen anything till you've seen a few hundred tiny *calaveras* dancing like mad, spilling out of their seats, arms around each other, feet beating madly against the earth. And all their lights shining out of them. Not small lights, not faraway twinkling stars, not half-hearted little lights, no, they were lights like those old fashioned Christmas lights—big and warm and soft. Like embers.

We had our own tour bus to take us around. Little electric things. We tried not to drive unless we were going from one small town to another, when it was safest to go at night, clinging to highway shoulders, though we tensed up every time a Big World car came close to flinging us off the asphalt. We became masters of hitching our little bus to Big World vehicles. Though sometimes it was just easier to mail ourselves somewhere or go in the luggage compartment of a Greyhound. Or to get a ride with somebody from the Cempasúchil Network. That's what we called it anyway. There were a lot of people in the Big World who knew we existed. They helped all the time in all kinds of ways. They called us Little Ancestors. There were those that provided space for us to live and create. Those that fed us. Those that transported us. Those that provided paint and canvas. Anything and everything we needed from the Big World that we would have trouble getting for ourselves. They were there for us every day of the year, not just on the Day of the Dead. They protected us and the secret of us. I think some of them prayed to someday become one of us.

It took us forever to find our name. We had about thirty songs we could play, most of them by Los Tigres del Norte. All the ones everyone always asked for: "La puerta negra," "La jaula de oro," "La banda del carro rojo" and some of their newer ones, like "Golpes en el corazón," "La mesa del rincón" and my personal favorite, "Eres mi buena suerte." We tried all kinds of names: Los Pumas del Norte, Los Jaguares del Norte, but everything was already taken. Panteras, Leones, Tigrillos, Linces, Leopardos, Guepardos. Every single kind of big cat name was already taken. As for the "del Norte," we figured that Texas was pretty much the northernmost part of Mexico, so that's what we told everyone who asked if we were from Tamaulipas, Nuevo León, Coahuila or Chihuahua. We ended up choosing "Los Ocelotes" because it sounded kinda cool but also because it didn't seem like anyone had ever chosen ocelots. And the encyclopedia said they were native to southwestern US and Mexico. Just like us.

We decided we'd always wear jeans and black cowboy boots with white or black shirts and our *chaquetas* with LOS OCELOTES emblazoned across the back.

Those first days were heady. Booking gig after gig. We got offered a record deal. A small South Texas imprint, but it felt like the beginning of something big. Guale and I started writing our own songs. Heard ourselves on the radio for the first time. Shot a video in Laredo along the border.

That's how I met Yolanda. She was the video director's girlfriend's best friend. The girlfriend was going to play Tim's new love interest, and she'd convinced Yolanda to be his old love interest. I swear I heard her name and the song, "Yolanda," from Jaime y los Chamacos just started playing in my head. "When I saw you the first time …" The way she looked at me. "You know I love you, Yolanda, you know I'd die for you." And that was it. I was gone. I thought, *I've found my Donna*.

No one ever said it out loud. But then again, it wasn't the kind of thing people said. We just realized it one day. Small World wasn't forever.

Of all the celebrations there, Small World didn't celebrate births and didn't celebrate deaths. New people just appeared. The *calaveras'* light would dim quickly, and then they just disappeared. We mourned them, yes, but mostly it just drove us more fiercely. Drove us to pour more of ourselves into creating, into loving, into dancing, into being.

There was no way to know what the next world would bring. In the journey from the Big World to the Small World, we'd lost our flesh and our height. What if in the next world we lost our bones or our names? What if I lost my accordion or my songs or my memories the next time I died? There was no time to waste. There never had been … in this world or any other. It might have just been me, but I felt like we sounded even better dead than when we'd been alive. It must have been all the freedom that finally got me writing songs again.

I asked Yolanda to marry me a year after the video in Laredo. She said no. She had three weddings before she turned forty. None of those were with me. She ended up with one kid from the first husband. Two from the second. None with the third.

Danny, Stephanie and Robert grew up calling me Dad. She came back to me after the first husband cheated on her, back to me after she got bored with the second one, back to me after the third one found a younger wife. And like an idiot, I kept taking her back. Kept thinking we were meant to be, that in the end she'd stay with me. I never married. I mean, there were other women, and some of them lasted for years. But as soon as Yolanda needed me, I'd drop everything: women, jobs, cities. Even though she'd told me from the start I wasn't enough, that she wanted a man who wore a suit and tie to work. Wanted the lakefront house and the condo in the city and a villa somewhere in Europe. Not some no-name accordion player in a no-name band always on the road, she'd hiss.

Los Ocelotes del Norte never went big. Never became anything like our idols, Los Tigres. When we died, they were still going strong, five decades and still putting out CD after CD, winning Grammys left and right. They had a star on the Hollywood Walk of Fame. That one CD of ours didn't go much of anywhere—just something to sell for beer and taco money. Before we could record a second CD, everything just kind of fell apart. Tim wanted to go to California and get his PhD in Chicano Studies. Riche was on his fourth or fifth kid and his dad wanted him to take over the bakery. Chino said he missed Aracely too much and wanted to see his kids grow up. Guale and I tried our best to get the guys to still meet up and practice, take a gig now and then. I went back to singing lead but my voice just didn't have that thing that Tim's did. I worked with one band and another—a good accordionist can always find a place—but it was never like playing with Los Ocelotes. Every now and then I'd have to take a break away from playing. My parents were hit by a car soon after I graduated and were never the same. My sister had married and lived next door, but she had her hands full with her kids and her always unemployed husband. I put the accounting courses I'd taken in college to use, started my own little accounting firm and did my best to keep us all afloat.

But there was never anything like what it felt like to hold that accordion in my arms. To squeeze out the sounds of a limping, pealing, bleeding heart. Nothing that felt like making music with the guys. Nothing that felt like the roar of the crowd and the heat and the spin of bodies dancing, feet moving to the beat of our music. Nothing like being Los Ocelotes del Norte.

I guess the guys felt the same. We made our way back to each other in our forties. Tim was on sabbatical for a year. Chino's kids were in college or married with kids of their own. Riche had sold the *panadería* and finally gotten a vasectomy. Guale's latest boyfriend designed our new outfits. And almost twenty some years after we'd decided on our name, we headed back out on the road. For a short while anyway. Until that night.

I didn't think I'd fall in love after dying. But I met Alicia at a concert in Austin. It was one of those artsy warehouses on the East Side run by someone in the Cempasúchil Network. I saw her from afar, all golden and warm like candlelight. We were playing the Los Tigres song that never stopped being my favorite, "Eres mi buena suerte." Tim was singing his guts out and I was backing him up. She was in the front row, scream-singing with her eyes closed and her hands over her heart. I could see her shoulders moving left and right, her body turning in a half circle, as if the song itself was holding her close and tight.

She stayed until the very end. Stayed until the concert was over and we'd talked to all the fans. Stayed until we were headed out to find a late-night place for tacos and to watch the sun rise over the water. She took my hand before I was even able to say a word.

We love each other fiercely. Our lights are brighter than they've ever been. She writes her poems and I play my music and we greet each day in the Small World as the gift it is.

hibiscus tacos

There have been centuries where I've really missed having a body. I like this one. I've been in it for about twenty years.

It's in its fifties now and still sorting what that means. Not old. Not young. I have a *señora* face and *señora* hands—not smooth, slightly wrinkled, a little lived-in, but good. Still strong. Still enough energy for a good *parranda*, an all-night sing and dance and scream and fight and run. It's just that that night's followed by one day of intense pain and then a few more days of lingering pain. But that's okay. The body mostly forgets by the time the next party comes around.

I'd never been in the body of a woman with tattoos before. All this gorgeous color down both arms, huge hibiscus blooms of red and yellow and peach. From both wrists to the shoulders. It was irresistible. I added more tattoos after a few years. Vines twined around my ankles, swirling up my calves, bursting into bloom on my thighs and hips. I like loose, flowing clothing, but sleeveless tops and dresses reveal my arms and shorts or dresses with high slits show off the color on my legs.

Took me a while to figure out how to shop for this body. I mean, yeah, when you're nothing but bones you can wear whatever you want. Never have to worry if you're going to be able to zip that zipper or close that button. If this color or that one is better for your coloring. What shapes are most flattering. You throw on a red or black cloak, and that's it, that's the signature look.

It took only a few days for me to start changing Gloria's life. I didn't like what she'd made of it. I figured she didn't either or she wouldn't have committed suicide at thirty-two. I quit her job. I sold her apartment. I told her family I never wanted to see them again. I left Dallas and bought a little house in East Austin. Gloria had some money—which always helps, even in my case. I tried painting. I tried poeting. I tried learning yoga and then teaching it. I tried going back to school. Gloria had been an architect. I thought maybe I'd discover some of her drive and talent, but school wasn't for me.

I had a lot of spare time. After all, I'd been me for a long time. It doesn't take much to review the petitions, prayers and promises that come in each night. When you have power over space and time, life and death, well, it's nothing to say yes to this one or no to that one. I do what my gut tells me to do. I don't make lists. I don't do analyses. I don't do charts or spreadsheets or graphs. I decide. I give or I don't. I take or I don't.

But sometimes you don't want all your life to be about prayers and power. I found my way when I realized I wanted to do a good thing, to make a good thing. I was happy shopping at the market and finding the ripest tomatoes, the best lettuce, the most fragrant cilantro and the avocados begging to be squeezed.

So, I bought a food truck. Shone it silver. Painted hibiscus blooms on all sides. Put up a sign with the logo I designed, a taco with a red and yellow hibiscus bloom inside it. *Hibiscus Tacos/Tacos de Jamaica* surrounded in little lights. Found a good spot, set up a website, opened it up before the food truck craze hit its stride.

I make a little of everything. All the classics: *carnitas* and *fajitas* and shredded brisket and *nopalitos*. But what I'm famous for are my vegan *tacos de jamaica*. I keep it simple. Nine meat fillings. Three vegan. *Jamaica*. *Nopalitos*. And spinach, mushroom and *calabaza* cooked with tomatoes and onions. No flour tortillas at my place. All corn. White, yellow and blue. To make it look nice, I color-coordinate the parchment paper on the baskets: white paper for the blue tortillas, red for the yellow, green for the white. No packaged tortillas either. They've gotta be fresh. I found an old woman from Michoacán around the corner who didn't want to die yet. I gave her a job making my tortillas. Perfect handmade tortillas, with her handprints and everything. She brought in her *comadre*, who was dealing with breast cancer. Together, they make five hundred hot-off-the-comal tortillas for me on Fridays, Saturdays and Sundays.

This is Austin. People here lose their minds when they see a menu that says "gluten-free," "vegan," "organic," "free-range" or "dairy-free." I can sell my tacos at five dollars a pop. I'm open only three days a week, from 5 p.m. until I sell out. Got *horchata* and *limonada* and *agua de jamaica*, too. I've known few things as satisfying as working with my hands, shaping order after order and feeding people, watching them smile. They close their eyes after the first bite and pat their bellies in happiness.

I've even got my regulars. Carlos and Roberto and Juanito come by every night I'm open and either bring their work buddies or their new girlfriends. They endeared themselves to me after that first night they showed up drunk and serenaded me with a surprisingly harmonious rendition of "Malagueña salerosa." Turned out they idolized Los Panchos. I told them they should go for it as musicians. They get free tacos in exchange for playing live two hours every Saturday. Now they're booked up for birthdays and engagement parties and weddings. I'm working on getting a couple of nightclub owners who love my tacos to come by on a Saturday.

Then there are all the Mexican laborers who come by and cry over the blue corn tortillas and the *el pastor* and the *nopalitos*. Anybody who cries over my food also ends up on my special discount program. Nothing like tears to make you feel like you're doing holy work.

Of course it was going to be Mexican food. That's been my favorite for as long as there have been Mexicans, and before that, the Aztecs and the Mayans and the Huicholes and the Otomi and so on. How could I help but love Mexicans? They love me best. Dress me in flowers and celebrate me and sing to me and pray to me like no one else does. I don't even have to be beautiful for them. They love me skeletal and they love me with scythes and, even more, they understand me. They know I'll come for them one day, and when it's their turn, they're among the few that never run. I'd prefer to take everyone that way—in a long, soft embrace.

They call me "Santísima." They call me "Flaca." They call me "La Pelona." Like I was their mother, their lover or their twitchy high school friend—never quite right but never excluded. Some of them still call me "Mictlantecuhtli" and "Mictecacihuatl" and make me offerings.

I didn't expect to love my little taco truck so much. To love the hours shopping, the hours cooking, the hours with customers, and even the hours of bookkeeping and cleaning and prepping. I guess everyone needs a change of pace sometimes. It'd been a while since I'd spent this much time in a body and since I'd been in love like that. Not since Kali. After the fall of Rome, we spent three centuries together, hopping from one body to another—man, woman, other—tripping over all the continents in turn. It was all made new because we were together.

Kali, well, I still don't know how to say that name without sighing. *Ay*, her hands. No one has ever had hands like Kali—hot as embers. I always marveled at waking without scorch marks on my skin. It didn't matter what body she was in; when she danced, no one else existed. I'll never forget what it felt like when she held me. How she could rage, her eyes flashing, her voice all growl and thunder. I've never had much of a temper, but she would push and push until I was throwing things against walls and screaming at her to get out. And then, one day, she left. Years and years later, when we saw each other again, it was as if we had never been.

Fourteen centuries alone convinced me that solitude was my way. And so, for fourteen centuries, I didn't even want a body, didn't want to miss the warmth of a body, didn't want to adore the tilt of a head or a crooked smile or a sigh behind my ear. When I became Gloria, I vowed I'd drink my fill of pleasure, taking lover after lover but leaving my heart out of it. After so many years alone, I wasn't sure I could feel anything anyway.

That resolution didn't last very long. I could feel Gloria's heart beating away in my chest, thumping and clamoring and clanging. She'd never been adored. In her whole life, her heart had never split itself open for another. What could I do when it drummed its need day and night? Okay, I said, I'll find some mortals to love. But only mortals. And I'll love them the way mortals can be loved. Partial loves. Fractional loves. Because they burn out so quickly. Because in a century or two, I'll barely remember their names. Because they'll love me incompletely, too. They'll never know who I am. They'll just remember me as Gloria. A woman with a painted body who was perhaps a little secretive but who loved like a firecracker, bright enough to light up the sky while it lasted. I could do that, I thought. I could live that way.

She had gray eyes.

It wasn't just that they were gray. It was that they held too much light. The longer I looked into them, the farther away she seemed. The first time she came to the food truck, she ordered three tacos, one of each of the veggie fillings, in passable Spanish. When I asked her what kind of tortillas, she said, "Whatever you think works best." So I made her hibiscus on white corn, *nopalitos* on blue, mushroom and spinach on yellow. I glanced at her every now and then as she ate them, rolling the tortilla slightly to safeguard the filling. Long slender neck. Light brown hair in a loose bun. Long limbs that should've been awkward but weren't. There was a concentrated stillness about her, so strong it seemed the air around her vibrated. No fidgeting. No people-watching. No scrolling through her phone. She ate her tacos. Breathed. Added a tiny bit of salsa. Otherwise, her gaze was turned inward.

I left the truck to wipe down and restock the little table where I kept a selection of lime wedges and cilantro and green and red and roasted salsas. I smiled and waved at a few customers that shouted their goodbyes. I felt her approach even before I saw her. She nodded solemnly at me, with a friendly expression but no smile.

"Thank you, she said, they were very good. I'll be back soon."

"Thanks for coming by," I said, just as solemn.

I watched her walk away and realized what it was about her stillness that had caught my attention. Living people were never still like that. She'd learned that stillness from the dead.

She returned a week later, early on a Thursday night. Wearing scrubs and a light jacket. She made the same taco order and added a lime Topo Chico. Again, that stillness, that concentration. I thought it would be another week before I saw her again, but no, she was back Sunday night.

It was oddly unnerving. That inward concentration had shifted. Every time I glanced in her direction, she was looking at me. Every time I caught her at it, she never blushed or looked away. Just kept her eyes on me. Direct. Warm. She came back up to the window to thank me when she was leaving.

She introduced herself, held out her hand, "My name's Laurel. I can't thank you enough. You make the best tacos I've ever eaten in my life."

There were laugh lines around her mouth and traces of crow's feet bracketing her eyes, but still no smile.

I took her hand, startled by how cool it was. Looked up at her. "My name's Gloria Paniagua."

"That's okay," she said, her hand tightening. "You don't have to lie to me. I know who you are." She paused, withdrawing her hand to pull a note out of her pocket. "I brought this for you."

I took it without touching her hand. Thick white paper. Folded once. An inky pen. Five names. Three women and two men. Dates of birth. Room numbers. *@Isaiah House* written beneath the names.

"What's this?"

"They all need you. If you can visit them tonight, you should."

I took a step back. Leaned against my truck, waited. She didn't turn away, didn't look down. Her eyes were so clear.

"What? No pleading, no bargaining, no praise?"

"No. You'll be taking them anyway. I'm just asking you take them a bit sooner. Ease their pain."

She turned and walked away. Back straight. That same measured long stride.

I didn't think I was going to go, but I did. Easy enough to find Isaiah House. Why use immortal powers when you have the internet? My phone even gave me hours and directions. I parked a few blocks away, even though there was plenty of parking at 3 a.m.

When I'm in a mortal body, I like experiencing time and distance like a mortal. Day and night. Minutes and hours. Weeks and years. Decades. A block is a block, and gravity is gravity, and I stop at stop signs and—mostly—keep to speed limits. I don't push my mortal body to do things it's not designed to do. No flying or becoming invisible. You can't leave a mortal body alone for more than a few minutes. No way to avoid brain damage, you know. The body starts twitching or going numb or forgetting how to speak. And it's a pain in the ass to have to start all over again, in another body, another life.

It's also quite boring to spend an eternity running around, visiting mostly terrified people to give them the cold touch. Six thousand people around the world die each hour. Sure, I could disregard time if I shed Gloria's body. But I'm not ready to do that. And truthfully, that's an exhausting way to live. I figured out a long time ago that delegation was the key. I send my _____s instead. Each region has a different _____. Every religion, too. New _____s join us all the time. It's important to stay updated and relevant. Otherwise, people don't believe capital-D death has come for them. Give people what they want, what they expect, and they'll follow you, even into the Other World.

I have weekly meetings with my _____s. Well, not all of them, just the seven continental managers. I make a huge pot of *pozole* and chop up the garnishes. Or dozens of *enchiladas de queso fresco* and a big pot of beans. They love my pretty pomegranate ceviche. My *nopalito* salad. I bring out my pretty blue and white *talavera* pottery and order fresh flowers from the florist down the street. Dahlias whenever possible. Gladiolas in all colors, each in their season. Sunflowers. We gather. We eat. They report. I make *cafecito* and send someone down the street for *pan de polvo* from the bakery next door to the florist. I don't know if anyone loves good food more than the dead. They find subjects to discuss until it's time for seconds.

All of this to say, I was good in Gloria's body. I didn't see any reason to leave it for even a few minutes. So, I went in her body to Isaiah House. The doors were unlocked. I walked into what looked like a large community living room. Tables and comfy couches. Children's books and board games piled up on the coffee tables. The golden light of the large lamp in the corner made everything glow. A hallway. Faint murmur of voices. I passed by a room that seemed to be emitting a soft purple glow. The sign by the door read *Serenity Room*. I peeked in. Blues and purples everywhere. Stained glass that couldn't reveal its true colors in the darkness.

I felt a sudden heat flush along my side and turned. She came close enough to touch me but didn't. Her hands rested calmly at her sides. Her eyes were as solemn as ever, but not dark. Not shadowed. Not haunted.

"This way," she murmured.

The woman at the information counter didn't even look up when we passed by. Laurel was five or six inches taller than me. I quickened my steps to match her stride. Lavender scrubs today. Her hair in its usual loose bun.

The hospice was one long hallway. More blues and purples. Each door a soft off-white, each with a hard plastic sleeve listing the patient's name. Laurel reached to open the door.

I placed my hand on hers. "I'm fine from here on my own."

She nodded, withdrawing her hand. "I didn't know you would come in person."

"Of course, I would. It's not very often I'm personally invited."

She tilted her head, shook it slightly and then walked back toward the counter.

The door opened easily. I stepped inside and closed it gently behind me. There was a woman drawing shallow breaths on the bed. A small mountain of pillows propped her up. The light from the bathroom, with its half-open door, was enough for me to see that she wasn't very old. Mid-to-late forties. Her thinning hair only just starting to gray. Her face too narrow, too sunken-in. It was too easy to see the lines of her skull. A young girl, no more than twelve, sat beside the bed, head resting on her folded arms. She whimpered in her sleep.

It wouldn't take more than a second. I paused and breathed deeply. It all welled up, the stars and the millennia, the pulse of a heart and the coldness, all flaring up inside me. I reached out to touch the woman's forehead. She took one last long breath. Exhaled. Was still.

I watched for a minute. The girl stopped whimpering. In her sleep, she reached for her mother's hand and held her own face with it.

I slipped out of the room.

No one in the hallway. Onto the next room. Not even ten minutes to go through Laurel's list. They were all asleep or unaware of their surroundings. None of them resisted. Or stirred. They released their lives with relief.

Neither Laurel nor the other woman were at the counter when I passed by on my way out. I sat in my car for a while, the radio on, the heavy thrumming beat of reggaeton reassuring me.

I may be able to do my work quickly. I may have done it for my entire existence. But that doesn't mean I don't mourn them. That—even in a single touch—I don't hold them fast to my heart and know them and love them with everything I am. I saw their whole lives, their brightness and their flaws. Three of the five had family members in the room. Had blankets and photos brought from home. Two of the five had been utterly alone, with no belongings that hadn't come from the hospice.

There were no beeping alarms, no flashing lights, no intrusive IVs or tubes or oxygen masks. They all simply stilled. No one would know what had happened until nurses stopped by on their routine checks or family members woke from sleep. These were the quietest minutes, before anyone knew they were gone. All five gone softly. How most mortals say they'd like to go.

I don't remember how I began, only that I was there at the beginning. Before breath. Before light. Before anything beat or moved or walked or thought. Before life, I was there. And when life came, I was still there. In the oceans, I swam with the smallest invisible things and the great beasts. Followed the animals to the land and the sky. In my memory, those billions of years are like a dream. The last quarter of a million are much clearer, but human minds balk at so much time. I try not to think of time in this way when I'm in a mortal body. They can comprehend the idea of billions or millions, but they can't know it. Knowing it would overrun the physical capacities of their brains.

So, I sat in the car and listened to J. Balvin and Bad Bunny and tried not to think thoughts about eternity or infinity or my place in the chaos of the universe.

Saturday night the boys showed up to play music. They finally had a name: Trío los Crisantemos. I told them pretty much anything else would have been more catchy. Trío las Calaveras. Trío los Cempasúchitl. Trío Juan Carlos y Roberto. Anything other than *crisantemos*. They just laughed and launched into a lovely three-part harmony version of "Solamente una vez." That succeeded in distracting me, because I started reminiscing about having once heard it sung by Agustín Lara himself.

It was a busy night, the line stretched fifty long and no one seemed inclined to give up despite the wait. I had Isela, one of the granddaughters of the tortilla-making *comadres*, taking orders. I didn't see Laurel, but I heard her order. I knew which tacos were hers. I added an extra wedge of lime and a few avocado slices to her plate. Who doesn't like a little extra avocado?

She waited until the line ended, until the music stopped, until Isela left, until I shut down the truck and turned off the last light. I met her eyes and said not a single word. What a solemn-eyed woman. How to explain how it drew me? The clarity of her. The lean smoothness of her walk. How strong her hands seemed. How she looked at me: too calm for heat, too direct for coolness.

"Thank you."

I shrugged, "It was nothing. As it was, they didn't have too much longer to wait."

"I know. It's just that they were in so much pain. I wanted to ease it. Pain doesn't understand time. Pain is an eternity."

I looked at her then. Saw what I hadn't seen before, too preoccupied with her strength and grace. Saw the lines of care, but also the lines of pain bracketing her mouth, carving the crow's feet at her eyes a little too deep.

For lack of a better way to say it, all living things have an expiration date. I could extend or shorten the amount of time as I liked, but the greater balance had to be maintained. A longer life for one meant a shorter life for another.

Some humans live almost their entire lives in complete ignorance of their mortality. Others recognize it acutely every day, every hour. It wasn't just because Laurel was a hospice nurse that she understood; she had come close to dying. She'd been so overwhelmed by the pain that she'd prayed to die. No wonder her voice had sounded familiar from the very beginning.

I raised my hand slowly, giving her time to move away, and my fingertips touched the line of her jaw. "I see now, that's why you're not afraid of me."

"I prayed to you," she said, brushing her lips over my fingertips. "Every time you told me it wasn't time yet. You were always there with me. When I lay in the dark alone. When I didn't know if it was my last day, my last hour. When the pain was too much."

I took a step toward her. As close as I could without our bodies touching. Close enough that I could feel the heat of her body making my skin flush.

And then she leaned toward me, her hands rising to touch my face. "I know this isn't the real you, but you're still beautiful."

"After twenty years, this is as much my body as any ever was. Besides, it's hard to do this when you're a skeleton," I said, touching her lips with my own. So soft, so warm.

She came by on Thursdays and Saturdays. Brought me new lists. Always thanked me. I'd stop by the hospice with food and herbal tea. Her coworkers became accustomed to seeing me come and go. Laurel waited for me on nights the taco truck was busy, sat with me at one of the picnic tables when it was slow. She befriended Los Crisantemos. Started mentoring Isela, who it turned out was studying to become a nurse. I stopped charging her for her tacos, and always added extra avocado. Found out she liked caramelized onions and made them just for her.

She told me stories about growing up in the Rio Grande Valley. "Ah," I said, "that's why you don't speak Spanish like a white girl."

"My nana was Mexican," she chuckled, "and my best friends were, too. I was six or seven before I figured out which language was which. I used to drive my Nebraskan-farm-girl mother crazy 'cause she couldn't understand me."

I told her about the ancient creatures of the ocean and the Black Plague. She told me about moving to Austin for her first nursing job. I told her what it was like to live in Gloria's body and how I could slow time. She told me about her Grandma Ruth, who she'd idolized and whose hand she'd held in the hours before she passed.

It was only with her that I realized how much I'd lived in Gloria's body as if it were a costume, as if it had come with its own persona. Before Laurel, my mortal lovers had never known I was me. I'd spent every minute holding back, working to not give away too much. I'd tried so hard to be who they thought I was, who I'd told them I was. And even my immortal lovers had never looked at a body of mine like she did. As if it were divine. As if it were inseparable from me. She'd reach to touch my hand, press the length of her leg against mine, lean against me when I made her laugh.

I liked it. The caution in her. How she came closer slowly, as if I was a deer and she wanted to feed me from her hand. Or sometimes, judging by her eyes, as if I were a ravening tiger and could take her head in a sudden lunge. She was six inches taller than me and probably outweighed me by thirty pounds but she never took her eyes off me when she approached. Which I also liked. I didn't need a mortal without the instinct for self-preservation. I didn't want one that would just fling herself at my feet and promise to do my will for all eternity. She made me want to know why she'd lost her fear, how she'd reconstructed herself out of stillness, how she could be a mortal and be so solid, immutable, as if she weren't made of flesh and bone and a paltry number of years.

It was another Saturday night. The truck had shut down, but a few customers lingered. Los Crisantemos were having a ball mixing up old-school *boleros* with country songs and Lady Gaga. (Trust me, you haven't lived until you've heard bilingual versions of "Shallow" and "Angel Flying Too Close to the Ground" sung in English and Spanish by three drunk brown dudes with guitars.) The night was lovely, the sky clear, the breeze cool. Somebody had brought mezcal and the edges of everything were fuzzy and bright.

Laurel reached to take my hand, but I wrapped my arm around her waist instead and laid my head on her shoulder, nuzzling her. I felt her surprise, but she leaned in close and put her arm around my shoulders. I got up to get us a round of Topo Chicos and lime wedges. When I came back, she was straddling the picnic bench, hands on her knees, twisting her torso to the sides with deep sighs. I handed her one of the bottles and sat down beside her before she'd done more than lift the knee under the table. I tucked in against her until I was leaning my back against her chest, my head on her shoulder.

She scooted forward until her thighs were bracketing mine and one hand was just barely touching my hip.

Sometime after 2 a.m., all the songs went classical and mushy. "Bésame mucho" and "Amorcito corazón" and "Solamente una vez" and "Usted." Even drunk and half out of their minds, the boys didn't miss a single chord or a single chance to harmonize.

Laurel's hands slowly moved up, until she'd locked them around my waist.

"Usted me desespera, me mata, me enloquece," they were singing when she leaned in close. "I want to watch you," she murmured, her lips skimming along my neck.

I said nothing. She knew I was saying yes. Before long, I called a cab for the boys and gave the driver Roberto's address.

Laurel came with me. She barely waited until I'd parked the car, locked it, disarmed the burglar alarm and opened the front door. I turned to welcome her to my home. Not a single word made it out. Her back thudded as it hit the wall, and she used her long arms to pull me toward her. All teeth and heat. Nipping and gnawing at my bottom lip, my earlobe, my shoulder, the fleshy parts of my hand.

"I want a shower. I smell like tacos and kitchen cleaner and grease."

"Let's go."

We stripped our clothes as I led the way to the bathroom. I can't say who turned on the water or who poured the body soap or whose hands washed away the sweat and corn tortilla scent from me and the antiseptic scent of the hospice from her. I can't say whether she drew away or which one of us said, "Now."

Because then it was now, and she'd moved away. She watched me. Her eyes so clear and intent. I wondered how she'd known to ask for my favorite thing. I'd always loved watching my lovers without touching them. To see them peel themselves open. The first deliberate touch. The tremble of thighs. The arched backs and feet pushing against floors and cushions and walls and beds. The eyes heavy and the *oh fucks* and *oh gods* and other words they stuttered over. The slack jaws, the winces, the whimpers, the mewls, the moans, the catches of breath, the screams, the groans. What I wanted was the truth of them—what was raw and honest. I didn't want the practiced looks of seduction, the careful poses, the clenched abs, the unoriginal porn-inspired monologue.

So, I gave her what I'd always wanted. The truth of me. Every touch, every pleasure, every sound. Her eyes drank me in. And even when it was all too much and I closed my eyes, I opened them after and found her eyes still looking into mine. As if she wanted to see into the untouchable of me, the eternal of me.

She put two fingertips to my lips, so light I barely felt them. "So beautiful. You, the goosebumps on your skin, all of the petals of your tattoos flushing red, the slick of you, but then you waver and I see the polished bone of you and then I see the night sky and the stars of you."

"Come here."

Her mouth. I needed to taste her mouth again. One of us shut off the water. One of us grabbed towels. One of us led the other to my bedroom. One of us whimpered, or maybe it was both of us. The collision of bodies isn't always all hands and nipples and cock and cunt. What lingers in the mind, on the body, is this. The warmth of a hand. The testing of muscle. Fingers measuring a wrist, an ankle. Desire sweeping along a calf, kneading a thigh. Breath against shoulder blade. Eyes that never leave you. The weight of a body against yours. Not alone. Never alone again. What is offered, what is given and what is received. The world small and the light expanding. Laurel. The sight and sound and scent and taste and touch of her.

I woke up with her breath on my neck. Her arm tight around my waist, her small breasts pressed against my back, one of her legs between mine.

"Good morning," I said.

I felt her lips smile against my skin. And that was it.

Years have gone by. I still make tacos. I decided I didn't want a brick-and-mortar restaurant. Just more food trucks. Got half a dozen in Austin and looking at possibilities in San Antonio and further south. Everybody's loving the vegan, gluten-free, dairy-free options now.

Laurel is still a hospice nurse. I gave her the power of the cold touch a while ago. Not that I didn't want to come by the hospice to see her in the middle of the night. It just seemed more efficient to let her do it. After all, what makes more sense than a hospice nurse with the power to ease her patient's suffering? Well, I gave her more power than that. She could quicken their passing or extend their time a bit. Two weeks in either direction. The Austin regional manager of my ____s nearly shit himself when I introduced him to Laurel and told him he was now her manager. Poor guy's been freaking out with me being in town for all this time.

Laurel moved in. We got married. Los Crisantemos played at our reception. They're up for a Grammy for their first album. I got my last tattoo on our first anniversary. Purple mountain laurel blooms on my left shoulder blade.

I figure I can get in another forty years in this body. Forty years, seven months, two days and six hours to be exact. I set the timer on Gloria's body for the same time as Laurel's.

Maybe we'll be sleeping, curled up into each other, and between one breath and another, we'll both let go. Maybe we'll both take a bottle of pain pills, take a last swallow of water and reach toward each other, ready to leave but taking a last moment to look into each other's eyes. Maybe we'll go out in a blaze of glory, two white-haired women on motorcycles, screaming fiercely as we drive off a cliff and aim for the sky.

xoxōtlameh, my love

When I think of my mother, I remember the fireflies. Late spring. Dusk. She'd hold both my hands, and we'd dance among them. "This is happiness," she'd shout and pull me up into her arms, spinning and spinning. We'd crumple laughing onto the grass.

"*Luciérnagas*," she'd say, pointing them out. "That's what they're called in Spanish, but my grandmother called them something else: *xoxōtlameh*. See how beautiful they are when they're flying around? All that light. But see, look close at that one. Without its light, it's just an ugly little bug. So let them fly so they can be beautiful. If you catch them, son, let them go right away."

She died when I was five. In one moment, I lost both my mother and my face.

I think of you when I walk. I've thought of you every night since I first saw you dance at the plaza. It's been months. It was in the spring. I'd seen the *danza del venado* a dozen times, but I'd never seen anyone dance it the way you did. A deer head with its antlers on your head, a loincloth, *ayoyotes* around your ankles, a red gourd rattle in each hand. Your black hair, thick and water-straight, loose and flowing down to your waist.

I was transfixed by the coil and stretch of the muscles in your arms and legs, the way your ribs flexed as you panted, your deer body frozen as it sensed the hunters approaching.

I take a walk every night at this hour, late enough that there is little traffic. The fireflies are long gone, though it's still warm. Doesn't feel like the calendar will be saying winter soon. I stay in my neighborhood, avoiding the brighter lights of the main streets.

It takes more than I have to leave my house bare-faced. It takes more than I have to let people see what happened to me. And so I wear the mask. I carry a note from my doctor that explains the need for it. A letter from the chief of police to keep me from being arrested. A 6-foot-2 brown skinned man with a mask doesn't tend to go unnoticed. I've been pulled over by cops, tackled to the ground and taken to the police station too many times to count. When it's not the cops, it's other men—black, white, brown, doesn't matter. Even when I hunch my shoulders and try to look smaller, try to look like I'm not challenging anyone, they start calling me or pass by and check my shoulder.

As much as I can, I avoid outings. Even before the pandemic, I had my groceries delivered. Did all of my banking and shopping online. I have always worked from home. There was enough insurance money when I was a boy to hire my own teacher. I took as many college classes online as I could. It was a misery when I had to go in person. I didn't want anyone to see the scars, my twisted lips, the prosthetic for my jaw. You'd think they'd all avoid me, look away. But the stares followed me everywhere I went. And the incessant questions. Why the mask? What happened? What does it look like under there? Does it hurt? Couldn't the doctors do anything? Can I see? Can we see?

And the girl. It was always the girls who would reach to touch. One hand on my chest and the other reaching upwards. I couldn't smack their hands away, and it drew too much attention to leap backwards. I learned to keep my distance. My grandmother would ask, almost every day, if I'd made any friends. "Because," she'd say, "life is too long if you're alone." But when I was alone, there were no eyes on me. And nothing was wrong with me. Even my grandmother who loved me would look at my bared face with pity. Pity edged with horror. Doctors and nurses and techs tried not to show any reaction at all, but I could always see that almost imperceptible flinch before the return to the professionally shuttered expression.

Everyone has been wearing masks now, off and on, for more than three years. They say we don't need them anymore. But while it endures, my life is different. Because wearing a mask now means I'm careful, not monstrous.

I have masks in three colors: blue, black and brown. The brown gives people the least pause. From a distance, it hardly seems like a mask. Almost the same shade as my skin.

flutes and
drums and
rattles first

then two hunters
criss crossing space

arms and
legs flung
up

entreating

One night a year, I seek out the crowds. Put on a mask and know no one will look askance at me. In my earliest memories, my mother would take me to celebrate the Day of the Dead at the plaza. After she passed, I'd go with my grandmother to the plaza, where there would be music and food and poetry and flowers and *danzantes* and *altares* for blocks around. That year and every year, we'd placed a silver-framed photo of my mother on the communal altar along with an armful of marigolds and a white candle. After my grandmother died, I returned every year with both their photos, an armful of marigolds, and two tall white candles. With time, I added strawberry jelly rolls for my mother and *marranitos* for my grandmother. The photos in their silver frames would always be there when I came to collect them. The sweets never were, but it didn't matter if children or spirits or the hungry had taken them. It only mattered that I'd offered them to their memory.

I went that night, knowing you'd be there. I wanted to watch you dance again. I readied myself carefully. I wanted to be one of the many in the plaza but also wanted to catch your eye. White paint over my whole face. Black paint over my brows, following the curve of bone around my eyes, dipping slightly downwards following my cheekbones. A white mask. Black over my lips. Black over the tip of my nose. The silhouette of a crow over the prosthetic. Then the crimson paint. Tiny stitches embroidering the edges of my face and along the lines of my covered scars. I freed my black hair from the short ponytail I kept it in, streaked it with silver and red. Black long-sleeved guayabera embroidered in red. Black pants. Black boots. My mother's blood red rosary around my neck.

I know you like men. If only I had another face, I would have gone up to talk to you the first time I saw you. Would have wanted to make you laugh. Would have wanted your eyes to look up at me then down with interest. I would have asked you to dance. Would have asked if you wanted a drink. Would have asked you to let me take you anywhere. If I had another face, I might have met you here at the plaza, at a bar, at a club, at a party. Maybe your friends would have known my friends. Maybe we would have passed each other on the street, seen each other and not been able to look away.

I saw you from afar as the first *conjunto* band was taking the stage. Your waist-length hair loose. Black and white *calavera* makeup on your face with marigolds painted over your eyes, marigolds braided into your hair. You were wearing a long-sleeved pale-yellow tunic that revealed your collarbones, that dipped low to reveal the smooth expanse of your muscled chest. I didn't tell my feet anything, but they found their way to you. I didn't say a word, just held out my hand to you, everything I wanted to say in my eyes. And you took my hand and folded yourself into my arms as if you'd been there a thousand times before. There was no hesitation, no stumbling, no awkwardness of deciding whose hands went where. My hand at your waist and your hand on my shoulder and we breathed in together and exhaled and took the first step as the accordions wailed. I didn't speak and neither did you. I concentrated on the music, on the beat, on the feel of you, on our bodies so in sync we barely brushed against each other. Your head had fallen back and your eyes were closed and you were smiling softly. I pulled you tighter.

To speak would have ruined it. You were a dancer. You wanted to dance, not to fend off my clumsy flirtations. And I didn't care. I'd dreamt that moment a million times, but nothing had ever prepared me for you in my arms. For the way it felt for our steps to match so precisely. For the barely-there scent of your cologne. For the sway of your dark hair. For the scent of the marigolds I crushed. There was a fine sheen of sweat on your face and your neck. I longed to taste it. We were impossibly close. I could feel your heart beating inside my chest. This was the dream: to move without thinking. To turn with you, to spin with you, our hands parting and meeting again and again. To breathe and not breathe. To become two bodies and music and nothing else.

The band went from a polka to a *cumbia* to a *huapango* to a *bolero*. You never pulled away and I never let go. Not until the music ended. And then came the final step and then stillness. You opened your eyes. Our hands came apart and we took a step away from each other.

"Thank you," I said and then fled.

the deer enters
leaps
runs stills
leaps

breathes

limbs of flesh and bone
all strength all grace

and then a sound that isn't wind
a scent that doesn't belong

You must have looked for me. You didn't call my name. I hadn't given it to you. There was just your hand on my shoulder, and I knew it was you. I'd knelt to wipe petals and other debris from the two silver-framed photos so I could wrap them and put them back in my leather bag. I looked up and saw your eyes of lambent gold. I was never going to do anything but follow wherever you led.

Is this real? Is this real? Is this real? I asked myself, not sure if I was dreaming or awake. Not sure if I had crossed over the line that marked one reality from another.

"Come here," I heard. "Come home with me," I heard. I don't remember cars or roads, only walking with my hand in yours. I don't remember the house or the door. Only that I said, "Leave the lights off." I wanted to learn you by feel and taste and scent alone. If it was going to be my only night ever with you, I had to remember every moment. I wanted to remember it with my skin, with my tongue. Wanted to imprint your scents and your sounds on every part of me.

I don't remember taking off my shirt or my mask. My shoes or my pants. I don't know why I wasn't afraid. I didn't pause to think of your eyes on me. Of you flinching or drawing back in horror. Of your hands hesitating to touch my broken face, hesitating to touch my body scarred with deep ravines. I hadn't uttered a word, hadn't made a single promise, hadn't made a sacrifice of any kind. But there must have been a prayer beating in my blood. Because there they were. All at once. Swirling. Weaving patterns of light, beautiful and unpredictable.

I uttered their name, not yours. "*Xoxōtlameh, xoxōtlameh,*" as if I was giving thanks, as if their name was an incantation, as if we were beginning a ceremony.

They transformed me. Their lights spread over the scars spiraling across my face, across my chest, across my side. Their lights filled all the places where flesh and bone had been torn from me. They took my history of pain and rewrote it. Made me something more than misery, more than outsider. They completed me. And when my mouth closed on your flesh, my lips were whole. I tasted you and I tasted you. If the touch of the *xoxōtlameh* was cold or hot, you didn't say.

I touched the sharpness of your shoulder blades. It seemed to me that you should have had wings. I felt along the tight muscles of your back, your waist. I thought I'd known what longing for you was. But I hadn't known. I couldn't pull you close enough.

I didn't know you would be so light in my hands—so much muscle—but I lifted you so easily. Your thighs flexed under my hands. The thighs I'd seen leaping in the air. My hands spread across them, running along the firm muscle, kneading. My hands went downwards and inwards, seeking the flesh with give, with softness.

There was no way to ask you what you saw when you looked at me, what you felt when you touched me. Questions would have made the *xoxōtlameh* disappear. And even with the taste of you on my tongue and the harsh grunts we both made and the sweat on our skin, there was something holy in this descent into the body of another.

burning graze of an arrow
          too close
run
run
run
          too many hunters
                    run
                    run
                    run
every breath
        desperate now
                    too weak
run
run
run

I left when your eyes stayed closed and your breaths deepened. I had to go before the morning light came. Had to go before the *xoxōtlameh* left me.

Months pass. I manage to stay away from you. Manage to keep busy, do my work, watch movies, walk every night in directions that don't take me past your place. But then something reminds me of you. I see green leaves spilling over a wall, and they remind me of your eyes. I feel the wind on my skin and remember us spinning and spinning.

I begin to dance at night. In my backyard. In the dark early hours of the morning. Silent except for my breathing.

Winter comes. Spring comes. The fireflies return. Fireflies swooping together and apart in crazed circles and zigzags and patterns that seem random. But sometimes, if I stare at them long enough, it feels like I could one day understand them. You were a dream. You were a gift. The feel of you is seared into my skin. You don't know what you were to me. I won't seek you out again. You could never love me. And when I think that I want to howl, and if I could howl, I would howl until I tore out my throat.

I wonder what I am for—this unloved broken thing always in hiding.

But then the night comes again. The darkness comes again. The silent hours come again. And when I dance, the *xoxōtlameh* come.

a last arrow
deerheart drum
slowing
slowing
run
run
no more running

the earth is soft
a breath
a breath
a last breath

I feel it singing in my blood. This is why I was born. Even alone. Even unwatched. This is what keeps the world living. All of us dancing, alone and together. The deer is sacrificed. I am sacrificed. I rise again and the deer rises again. I breathe and the deer breathes. I run and the deer runs. I leap and the deer leaps. Earth. Sky. Wind. Bodies. Blood. Running. Alive. The deer and I are all these things.

The *xoxōtlameh* are always with me now.

with wings, hooves and horns

The babies have no interest in settling down to sleep. I still need to take care of a few things before I can close my eyes. It's been a long day. I'm so tired. My feet hurt, my eyes hurt, my head hurts. I'm too old for this. Of all the mothers I know, I'm the oldest with newborns.

They're growing fast. A little more than half made it this time. I think there were eighteen or twenty of them. I lost a few when they didn't make it into my pouch. Some of them didn't eat enough or went to sleep and never woke up again. I think they're old enough that it's safe to name them now. To learn the markings of their face and fur, to begin to distinguish their particular cries and yips.

It took three or four litters before I learned it was best to not get attached in the first days. I wept and wept over those tiny dead bundles of flesh and bone as they grew cold and colder. They smelled like *mine*.

I tell the young mothers what no one told me, "You have to make your heart hard to be a mother." There will always be a few that are too weak. A few that won't eat enough. A few that won't hold on as hard as they should. A few that will be eaten. And some you'll see to adulthood and then they'll be shot or hit by a car or any other number of things.

I don't know how many litters I have left in me. These might be my last babies. My body's slowing down. The males are all running after the younger females. I don't know how much time I have left. After these last ones are gone, it might be time to gather some food and stay in my burrow and just lay my body down. I don't think I'll ever want to get up again.

I wasn't as careful as I should have been. I was tired and it was late. There was no time to run. A bright light blinded me, and my body was hit with so much force that at first I didn't feel it, I only heard it. A tremendous pulse of sound tore my flesh away from my bones. I spared a thought to wonder if my babies would survive without me, and then everything went dark.

I didn't expect to ever wake up again. And if I had, I would have expected to wake up in excruciating pain, my body flung to the side of the road. Alone. Or being picked at by vultures. Not in this unknown place. No trees. No earth. No walls. Only a soft pulsing redness all around me. Streaks of light shooting through it like falling stars. I stretched my paw but the redness offered no resistance, and I saw that there was no paw. I had no body.

And then I realize I'm not alone.

"Hello?" the voice said, "Hello? My name is Pedro Linares López."

I made some sound that wasn't a word, that wasn't a greeting. I couldn't tell if what he'd said was humanspeak or animalspeak or which kind of either it was. I only knew that I understood him.

"Am I dead?" I asked when I could speak. "Are we both dead?"

"I don't know," he said. "I think we might be in Purgatory."

"I remember the white-white lights," I told him, not asking what Purgatory is.

I should be hurting. My body should be lying burst open on the road. My skull smashed. If I'm alive, how am I not screaming?

He says he can't answer any of my questions. He doesn't know anything. Only that he knew he'd fallen sick, that he'd taken to his bed for days without number. He says he cannot die yet, that his wife and his children are waiting for him to return. What will become of them without him? His mother's grief would be terrible to see if he were to die before her.

I wonder if I'm dreaming him or if he's dreaming me dreaming of him.

I realize he is a man before he realizes I am an animal. I don't think this is because I'm an animal and he's a human. I think it's because I pay more attention. And it takes him even longer to realize what kind of animal I am.

"*Tlacuache*," he asks.

"*A'brix'e*," I respond, thinking he wants my name.

Time becomes meaningless. I'm grateful not to be alone. We sleep sometimes, I think. He always starts awake, calling my name. I wonder how long he was alone, when I feel how relieved he is to hear my voice. He tells me about the laughter of his children, about the scent of his wife's hair. He tells me how he spent his days when he was in the world. Working with paper and carboard and paste and paint, creating piñatas and Judases. He says it's what his father taught him. And how much better he thought it was to create what his imagination envisioned than to till in the fields, to slaughter chickens or cows, to construct buildings, to make shoes or loaves of bread.

In exchange, I tell him about my babies, about the deep woods, about the vanishing wildernesses.

He tells me about the trees he climbed as a boy, the rivers he swam. We tell each other stories about the moon and the sun and the stars. About fish and insects and the heat of a summer day. We tell each other how we didn't know it was possible to miss having a body so much. Even our aging and tired bodies.

We are nothing alike. But it feels as if there are parts of us that are interchangeable. He tells me that most humans don't think animals have souls. I tell him I'd never known humans had souls, but it makes sense they would. After all, humans are animals.

I'm not sure when it began. He was a scent before he became a shadow. And then his shadow had the weight of a physical presence. We talked as we always did, measuring eternal time with our words. But then our conversations became marked with the moment I first began to see the movements of his hands, the moment his eyes were more than dark impressions, the moment I saw my own fur again, the moment I could again feel the rolling of muscles in my body.

It happened when he was telling me how much he missed working with his hands. That it didn't matter that most of what he made was either beaten to pieces or set ablaze. I listened to him talk and thought about my work of creating. My life had gone to surviving and eating and rutting and making babies and running and watching the sky and breathing and living.

I told him, "If I have an art, it's being."

It happened then. I looked and saw that my grey fur had a tinge of magenta. My legs were growing impossibly long, and electric blue stripes were stretching across them. I felt a weight on my back I'd never felt before and a group of unknown muscles. I flexed them and saw bright-yellow feathered wings extend and push against the red pulsing.

He reached out his hands as if to touch me, then paused.

For a second he disappeared, then just as quickly, reappeared.

"I think I'm waking up. I saw my home, my wife's face, the window by my bed." He held out his hands, palms up. My feathers brushed against them.

"The humblest creature of the wild," he said. "You are the art that wants to become, the medicine that wants to become."

Then, I was the one who disappeared. I saw the forest and the road. Flexed my golden wings and rose above the earth. In the next breath I was back in the red pulsing.

"Perhaps this is what we are," I told him, "each other's becoming."

We were solemn as we watched each other disappear.

So much gladness in my heart as I flew toward my burrow and found all my babies still sleeping. As I lay beside them and they gathered close to suckle, I watched them change, become more themselves. All the colors I'd ever seen and some I'd never seen before emerged on their fur. As they grew, I watched them all change. Wings emerged. And hooves. And horns.

When they asked what we were, I told them honestly, "We are medicine. We are art. We are what will always be becoming."

serpents-her-skirt

Live or not live. Die or not die. Die so that everyone lives. So that the darkness will not be eternal. So that the sun rises again. Live so that this is not the end of the story. Fourth fifth sixth sun, fourth fifth sixth world, every world and every sun are precarious. What do you weigh at the end and beginning of time? What is agony and what is sacrifice if your beloved world requires it?

What is the body when you are a goddess? When the light of the stars lives in your hands? When the blood roaring from your throat doesn't mean death? When the shattered limbs do not mean helplessness? The body has known pain. The body has known death. This body does not surrender. And so the body accepts agony and the body births agony. Births itself.

Sacrifice of godflesh. It is not a spilling of light but blood and red muscle and white bone and bile and *entraña* and weeping that is more fire than salt. Fountains and geysers and roaring oceans of blood all at once. Head taken. Limbs taken. The torso seizing, breasts laid bare. Hips convulsing and the godsex exposed. And time and no-time and before-time and after-time all collapsed.

This is the moment of origin. The moment of choice. When neither the name-before nor the name-after will encompass the story. Where the divine and the flesh meet implacable will. Because death is the end of effort. The end of pain. To live is infinite work. To survive is infinite struggle. To endure is an infinite cycling of pain. To transform an infinite act of creation.

The body chooses life and, choosing life, fountains of blood become serpents. Seize them, and two of their heads shall be your head. Two identical heads facing each other, infinitesimally close, infinitesimally distant, creating the illusion of one symmetrical serpent face. Transform or die. And your limbs now gone, also become serpent, also become talon, also become monster. What is monster in the face of the divine. Is not all the divine monster somehow to the human? Why fear the monster within? The divine made flesh is always monstrous.

Breathe. Blood made muscle. Fists clenched and relaxed. Flesh and stone. Face and stone. The heart is never stone. The heart is an infinite volcano of blood. Breathe and the body moves. Breathe and see that the world has not ended, is not ended, will not end. Breathe and see this body reflected and not. Breathe, and the serpent mouth, the sibilant serpent tongues whisper, "I am the mother of myself first."

How many are there? Serpents-her-skirt and hearts-her-skirt and stars-her-skirt and lightning-her-skirt and flowers-her-skirt and more. All the sisters. All the not sisters. Infinite and infinitely reflected. Tears and blood and godflesh and sweat and willing sacrifice and all the light within and the choice and the monstrous and the breathing and all the stars and all the serpents.

And this is how the world never ends.

song of the burning woman

Emma Elisa

I said I'd grow the flowers myself.

And I did. From seed. Now here they were, blooming everywhere, in every shade from lemon yellow to gold to orange to dusky red. Solid and striped. Some the size of bushes. Others fit wholly in my hand with the roots lying on my wrist. Every variation I'd been able to find: African, French, Signet, Tangerine Scented, Spanish Tarragon, Irish Lace.

The idea came to me last year when I was taking down my Day of the Dead altar. I hadn't built such an elaborate one in decades. But the silence and the isolation had seemed to call for it. No one had thought we'd still be social distancing last November. I don't count the months anymore. I only remember it was a March when the world moved from one kind of time to another, one kind of space to another, one understanding of death to another.

The days and the months and the years were like an accordion, flexing this way and that, speeding up and then slowing down. People got sick. People got better. People died. It was a weird thing at first, to be a woman without family in a pandemic. I never knew my father. My mother died when I was in my twenties. No brothers, no sisters, no close cousins.

No connections to elderly aunts or uncles. All those connections long gone. Left behind when I decided that neither hiding nor judgment were for me. I didn't know if they lived or died. Even before the pandemic, I'd sometimes search online for their names and add the word "obituary." As the years passed, there were fewer names to search.

I made my arrangements years ago. Before I retired. Went to the funeral home and laid everything out, paid for everything. My friend José said he'll deal with my art and Sol will take care of everything else. I'll leave no chaos behind me. Maybe my friends will gather, wish me well in the afterlife, pour a little tequila on the ground for me.

I've always loved parties. Loved the music and the colors and the people and their joy and the dancing and the food and the drinks. Loved the planning and the inviting and the way time ran swiftly at the start and then slowed syrup slow in the later hours. Loved those molten hours before dawn when only close friends remained and the brightness of the night glowed like an ember in my chest. I always loved my own parties best ... because hosting kept me busy when melancholy threatened. Because if I needed to escape, I forgave myself the need to make excuses.

I used to love dancing. When I was young, I could dance for hours, flinging myself from one partner to another or dancing by myself or as part of a vast faceless crowd. I never cared if someone was watching. Hell, sometimes I wanted everyone to watch. It never mattered to me as long as the beat compelled my body. When I grew older and one injury after another froze up my joints, the singing became everything. I'd sing until my voice turned to gravel, until it seemed my voice could fill the entire room, until everyone was singing with me, until I'd emptied out all the lyrics that lived in me. It didn't matter to me if I could sing or not or if other people were off key, what mattered was that we sang together.

My house is a little house. Nothing special to anyone but me. Corner lot. Eight-foot wooden fence for the backyard that I put in for my ex because she used to lay out naked whenever the sun was shining. Like a *pinche lagartija* trying to get her cold-blooded heart pumping again. She left me three years ago. No fights. No arguments. She was just done with me. I finally got all her stuff out of the shed behind the house. I took anything someone could still use to the battered women's shelter. Tossed the rest of it. I didn't burn it like my dramatic heart wanted, but at least it's gone now. Next time she thinks to call or text me and promises to come pick it all up, I'll tell her, "Nah, don't worry about it. It's gone." And she won't believe it. I know what she'll say. That I'm trying to make her hop on a plane and come see me. That I still want her back. She'll say it's because I never stopped loving her. That she knows she broke my heart and that I'll never be able to love anyone else again. But that's a lie. Only I know my capacity to love. And there's enough left for someone else. Enough love left for one more great love. Or maybe three little ones. Even though my hair's grey. Even though I've been retired for ten years. Even though my body is wrinkled and sagging and plump and scarred. But none of those things diminish me. I am more now than I have ever been.

It felt a bit odd to plan for a party again. I was cautious beyond cautious, waiting through pandemic waves. Years without drawing up lists and planning out the space and thinking of what I needed to build and who to invite. But even my cautious heart didn't want to wait anymore. It was time for a party. A small and lovely and long party. With talk and food and singing and dancing and art and photos. I asked Nora to make us tacos, and Sol brought *pan dulce* and a huge pot of *caldo.* José volunteered to make drinks. I stocked up on *chorizo,* bacon, eggs, potatoes and flour tortillas for whoever's still here at breakfast time. I cleaned and cleaned until not a speck of dust remained. I set up stations in the backyard—six large ones, seven small ones. Built them myself. They're not fancy—plywood and two by fours, hammered together with nails and prayers. And then I invited my friends to make *altares* of them.

I grew all the marigolds in anticipation of today. Marigolds along the fences and the house. Marigolds around the trees. Marigolds along the sidewalks. Marigolds bursting from My Lady. My Marigold Lady. Lady Cempasúchil. What else can I call her? She's a little bit of one thing, a little bit of another. Multi-hued marigolds bursting from her earthen flesh. A little Xochiquetzal, the goddess of flowers and art. A little bit of me. Somehow she has my mother's eyes. I built her thirteen feet tall. You can feel her serene gaze from every corner of the backyard.

José

It's an art. I told Elisa we weren't going to have that margarita mix shit from HEB. I brought all my own bottles and ingredients. Enough Patrón Silver to float us all away. My own syrups and fruit blends and garnishes. I had twenty-six specialties. One for every year Ismael and I were together. I didn't know it was going to become a tradition. Our first year, I invented El Mango Tango Wango Margarita and served it to him with *taquitos de chorizo y papa* in bed while singing "*No tengo dinero*" at the top of my lungs. That went over so well the next year, he got El Tierno Corazón de Melón Margarita with green salsa *chilaquiles* and "*Amor eterno.*"

The last time we celebrated an anniversary, he could barely eat or drink, but he sipped my Tulipán TinTan Te Quiero Mucho Margarita while I serenaded him with "*Yo no vivo por vivir*." At the time, I didn't know how little time was left. The oncologist had estimated a few more months, but it was only a few weeks.

This is my first Día de los Muertos without him. Elisa told me I could have one of the big *altares*, so I could do one of the big mixed media art and music installations I was known for. But that was "my work," and I didn't want to make anything that would be photographed and catalogued and written about. I didn't want to answer questions in the future about how important Ismael had been to me or what reaction grief transmuted into art should evoke in the viewer. I just wanted to remember Ismael. So I told her the kitchen counter would be all the altar I'd need.

Elisa had a ton of marigold bouquets and tall white candles all over the kitchen. I'd printed up a pretty little menu with all the drinks. And though they weren't expecting it, everybody got a little bit of a song with their drink: No Te Agüites Aguacate Margarita was served up with lyrics from "*El Noa Noa*," the Cucurrucucú Coconut Margarita with "*Querida*," and La Fresa Triste y Linda Margarita with "*La diferencia*." That last one almost made me break into tears, but then again, *rancheras* are supposed to make you do that. So if my voice wobbled, it wasn't more than anyone expected.

I lost track of how many drinks I made, how many times the blender whirred, how many oranges, pineapples, strawberries, limes, mangos and avocados moved through my hands. I spent my breaks eating the tiny little tacos Nora was making in the backyard with fajitas, *cebolla asada*, cilantro and lime. I'd have a Corona and then go tour the *altares* as they were being built. I restrained myself mightily as I saw people struggling with color coordination and their arrangements. I reminded myself that love has its own aesthetic, that they would all look beautiful by the time they were done. If nothing else, we could always add more marigolds.

When Elisa wasn't looking in my direction, I'd grab a quick marigold bloom and eat it. When we first saw *Monsoon Wedding* years ago, it awoke a ferocious hunger in me for marigolds. I won't eat the ones from florists because I know they're full of chemicals, but I could never resist them when I saw the edible flower petals at the grocery store. Or when I saw them in people's yards. They taste a little smoky, a little spicy, a little bit like a single paint-stroke of sunlight on the tongue.

There was a quiet hour, just as the sun went down, when everyone was busy finishing the last details of their *altares*, laying down flowers and food and photos. Candles were being lit everywhere—twelve-day candles in multicolored glass, patron saints everywhere, the Virgen de Guadalupe and the Virgen de San Juan vastly outnumbering everything else. Elisa was everywhere, handing out little ceramic plates and saucers in an effort to cut down the risks of everything exploding and catching fire and burning her house down to the ground. I don't know what it was, but an impulse seized me, and I took advantage of Mayra's arrival to uproot an entire bush of pretty striped marigolds that were growing in the backyard. Elisa never saw me since she was busy directing the lighting of the two-foot-tall beeswax candles Mayra had placed all around the Lady.

I plucked a pile of the deep green leaves and then pulled the petals free by the handful. I rinsed them and put them into two glass bowls with ice water. Under my breath I started singing, and it took me a few lines to realize it was the chorus from Juanga's "*Siempre en mi mente*." Orange and grapefruit and lemon and lime and generous handfuls of marigold petals and this and that went into the blender. I was this close to pouring in some of the tequila when I suddenly thought of the three bottles of mezcal I'd brought to drink with Elisa and Kimberly. We always had mezcal when we were together, a tradition dating back to when we'd all been young artists in San Francisco. I'd brought three bottles of Del Maguey Vida Mezcal. I'd planned for us to drink one by morning and to gift them the other two, but I couldn't resist. Its smokiness would complement the marigolds like nothing else.

How to explain what happened with that first sip? The feeling I felt … like there was a small candle burning bright in my chest and its glow was growing and growing. I sang louder and louder and I didn't even know I knew all the words to the song. I thought of how much Ismael would have loved this gathering, how he would have taken up a spot close to the Lady and strummed his guitar, breaking into song throughout the night. How he would have come to the kitchen to see what I was making and then laugh when I'd catch him stealing my fruit garnishes. How he would have wrapped his arms around my waist and leaned in close to press a kiss behind my left ear. I thought for a moment I could see his reflection in the kitchen window and feel his beard stubble on my neck. I thought perhaps he hadn't really left me all alone. I salted the glasses and poured in the golden mixture and sipped it and for a moment tasted his lips again. I sighed and named it … the Cempasúchil Siempre Margarita.

Nora

I brought Miguelito's favorite toys. His stuffed elephant that I'd named Don Policarpio and that he'd called DonPio. A dozen little green army men, a jumble of Legos, his soccer ball. All the toys he hadn't been able to take with him when his grandfather took him.

I brought all the snacks he'd loved when he was little: a bag of Doritos, chocolate M&M's, the Mexican cookies with the pink and white puff marshmallows and coconut. Orange Fanta. I wasn't there to see what he kept on loving, what he outgrew, what new things became his favorite things. Every gift I ever gave him afterwards was a guess.

I had other things of his to add to the altar. His favorite jacket. His watch. The photo of a pretty dark-skinned girl that had been under his pillow. When everyone was at the funeral, I broke into the house and took those things. They were mine to take. Everything was mine: the scent of his pillow, the imprint of his feet in his shoes, the thick dark strands of hair in the comb on his nightstand.

I took the framed photo my mother had of him in the living room.

I noticed every trace of me had been erased. Even after all this time I could see the darker places on the wood paneling where I remembered old family photos had hung. The photo of me and my two sisters on my tenth birthday. The photo of all of us that we'd taken at a special photography studio in Reynosa. My high school graduation photo. The photo of me in a high school football uniform. The photo of me at prom with Rosemary. All gone.

Back then, Rosemary had loved me as I was. It never mattered to her. I wore her clothes sometimes. She did my makeup and my hair. We did each other's pedicures and manicures. We'd kiss and taste Magenta Kiss/Red #578 on each other's mouths. We moved in together after high school and Miguelito came along before either of us turned twenty. My father wanted me to work with him, said I'd make more money in his shop than working as a waiter at Red Lobster. That one day

I could take over the business. But I wasn't stupid enough to spend any more time than I had to around him. If it hadn't been for Rosemary, I wouldn't have survived my teen years at home. In his eyes, the only manly thing I'd ever done was make his first grandson.

I worked all the time those first years. So I don't know when it started. Better said, I don't know when it started to get worse. Rosemary had always liked to party. She'd keep on drinking as long as there was something to drink. Would smoke or swallow or sniff anything anyone gave her. She cut down a lot when we moved in together. I think it was because we were both free of our families for the first time. And then she got pregnant. We were so happy. She worked a part-time job and spent that money on a crib and toys. When Miguelito was born, she stayed at home with him. Maybe that's when it started. But it wasn't until he was three that I'd come home after a double shift and find Miguelito eating a pile of Lucky Charms on the floor and Rosemary passed out on the couch. Beer bottles everywhere and the stench of pot in the air.

I started seeing some of our old friends from high school coming back around again. And all the signs were there. She was doing coke again. Taking whatever anyone gave her. We started fighting all the time.

At the same time, my mom kept calling and asking me to come by with Miguelito. Said it wasn't enough to see their only grandson on holidays and their birthdays. But it was just so hard every time we went there. Everyone at work and in our neighborhood knew me as Nora. Miguelito called Rosemary *Mommy* and me *Mamá*. He was too little to understand that everything had to be different at my parents' house. It wasn't like I could just wash my face and strip the nail polish off. I had to drill all these reminders into my head for days before every visit—how to walk, how to talk, what to say, what not to say, how to say it, how not to say it—to mirror my father's mannerisms, to take up space, to not show too much affection, to not take my plates to the sink, to say that Rosemary wasn't feeling well, to say that no, my mom and my sisters didn't need to come check on her or cook for me or watch Miguelito, that the drive from Los Fresnos was too far. Every time I left their house, I'd drive to the grocery store parking lot close to Business 83 and just bury my face in my arms and cry and cry with relief to have made it through. And Miguelito would cry with me.

My friend Ani stopped waitressing when she had her baby. She started watching Miguelito for me.

Rosemary and I kept fighting. And then she ended up in jail after she got pulled over when she was high. I got home one day after I picked up Miguelito, and all her stuff was gone. Things went to hell quickly after that. My parents heard from Rosemary's parents that she'd left. They came looking for me at work. Instead of Miguel Jr., they found Nora. They reported me to CPS for child abuse. They sued for custody. The judge called me a deviant in court.

I couldn't find an attorney who would take my case. I tried filing the paperwork on my own, but the judge had me declared a vexatious litigant after denying me custody and then visitation. My father threatened to shoot me if he saw me. My parents adopted Miguelito and had my name taken off his birth certificate.

No Miguelito. No Rosemary. No family.

I still tried to make a life, to be true to myself. I was Nora and never had to pretend to be Miguel Jr. again. I left Red Lobster and opened up a taco truck. After a while, I added a few tables, then a jukebox, cement to make a dance floor, a ceiling to shield people from the sun and the rain. Got a liquor license and sold beer.

I fell in love a few times. I had friends.

None of them knew I was also a ghost. That I watched my son from afar. Watched him go to school and run around outside during recess. Wondered if he cried for me before he fell asleep. Watched him as he grew taller and taller. Wondered if he remembered me at all.

And the years passed, and I had a little hope that maybe when he was eighteen and living on his own, I would walk up to his door and hold him again.

But I never did. An aneurysm took him when he was in high school. Even when he was dead, they wouldn't let me hold him.

Mike

Death's messed up. It's all these little flashes of lights. And memories. 'Buelo said he'd shoot him if he came around. But I just wanted to know him. Well, her, I guess. My dad. My mom. Whatever. They told me he was crazy and he'd hurt me if I went with him. It messed with my head. I saw him … her … everywhere I went. Sometimes during recess when I was a kid, she'd be parked in a car on the street next to the playground. When we'd go to the *pulga* or the HEB, she'd be following us, staying out of 'Buela's sight. I'd see her at church, six pews away, black lace over her face. I always knew it was her. I didn't know if she wanted to steal me away or what. Even though 'Buelo said his son was a pervert and a sin against God, I didn't get mad when I saw her. She made me sad. I thought about all my friends who didn't have their fathers no more, and I thought at least mine wanted me.

She'd leave little gifts for me in the mailbox on Saturdays. Small things nobody would notice. A little Hot Wheels car, a sack of marbles, some M&M's. When I got older, she'd leave a rolled up five-dollar bill, then tens, then twenties.

'Buelo and 'Buela were strict when I was little. I went to school, came home, did chores, did homework. Weekends went to more chores and church and big meals with all my uncles and aunts and cousins. The older I got, the more I looked like 'Buelo, and as long as I did what my 'Buelo wanted, I got to do what I wanted and go where I wanted. I got a driver's license and my 'Buelo's barely used Ford F-150 as soon as I turned fifteen. When 'Buela said I should be getting home before midnight, 'Buelo told her it was "*cosas de hombre*" and she needed to let me become a man, so I wouldn't turn out like the *desgraciado* her son was.

There were always parties to go to. Somebody's parents would be gone. There was an empty lot behind the abandoned gas station where we'd drink and hang out with our girls. I got into a few fights, bringing home a black eye or a few bruises. 'Buelo would only laugh and clap me on the shoulder the few times I came home a little drunk or a little bruised. He'd say, "See, he can handle his liquor and drive himself home fine" or "See, this one don't get beat down!"

I don't remember what my mom looked like. Or what her voice sounded like. Or how she smelled. But I remember crying and crying for my mamá. And how confused 'Buelo and 'Buela were because they kept telling me she'd left a long time ago. They threw away every photo that had either of my parents in it. Their names weren't even on the birth certificate that 'Buela kept in a zipped-up bank bag with her important papers. Mom never came to look for me, never called, never wrote, but I saw Mamá everywhere.

I didn't make the best grades in high school, and I wasn't on the football team or anything, but I had lots of friends and I never went more than a couple of days without a girlfriend after I turned twelve. I lost my virginity when I was thirteen. Never got anyone pregnant because I was careful. I'd heard too many times how my idiot father had gotten my whore of a mother pregnant and that if I hadn't looked so much like him, 'Buelo would have wondered if I was even his grandson.

I liked having girlfriends. I liked messing around with them, but none of them ever really made me feel anything. If one of them broke up with me, there was always another one waiting. If I saw a girl I liked more than the one I had, then I'd break up with that one and go around with the other.

Then I met Araceli. 'Buelo didn't like her. He said she was too dark, that I was a good-looking kid and I could marry White or at least one of those *rubias*, all blonde and blue-eyed, even though their last names were García or González or Reyna. But I thought she was the most beautiful girl I'd ever seen. She had the most beautiful eyes, a little slanted and a hot gold color. Her skin was dark and beautiful, so clear and smooth. She was so funny and a little bit of a smartass in class. She was always having to stay late for detention for talking back to the teachers, so I'd wait for her in the parking lot until they let her out. What I loved most about her, though, was that she was so *cariñosa*. None of my girlfriends had ever touched me like that. Most of them would put their hands on me like they wanted to show that they owned me. Or they'd wrap my arm around their shoulders or their waists like they wanted all my attention all the time. But Araceli would touch me softly, her hand on my arm or my shoulder, for just a moment. If I pulled her even slightly toward me, she'd cuddle into my side or sit on my lap. Without any shyness, she'd press little kisses next to my eyes, on my jaw, sometimes even on my hands. She'd run her fingers through my hair or drum the beat of whatever song was playing in her head on my chest.

The first time we were together, everything was so slow. There was no rush. No hesitation. The afternoon light was streaming in through the window. I kissed her eyes. I cupped her small breasts and marveled over her dark nipples. I memorized the scent of her. Before I leaned in to taste her, I parted her flesh with my fingers. So beautiful. The color like the *amaranto* that grew in our backyard. When she kissed me, she held my face with both hands. And even after we both came, her legs and arms were still tight around me.

She became my whole world. I told 'Buelo I was going to marry her. He called her horrible names and said I was too stupid to know what I was doing. He'd given me everything I had he said, and he could take it all back. I told him that if he couldn't respect her, I'd walk right out the door. He could have his pickup back. He could find someone else to leave his auto body shop to. I'd walk out the door naked if I had to, I threatened.

Next thing I knew, there was a bright light and a red wash of blood and then I was gone. I saw 'Buelo's shocked face for a split second.

I didn't take anything when I left my grandparents' house. Not even my body.

Araceli cried and cried for me. I pressed kisses against her eyes. I hope she felt them.

Sol

I asked if I could have one of the small *altares*. Elisa didn't laugh at me when I told her I wanted to make one for my little Luz.

Guillermo never wanted us to have a dog, so as soon as we split up, I went straight to the shelter. Luz didn't have a name yet. He was one of five puppies that had been brought in a few days earlier. He was puppy #3. It was love at first sight. He was sleepy and looked like a grumpy old man. A pretty golden color all over with the blackest eyes and nose. A white splash on his chest and neck. "*Luz de mi vida*," I thought. He was going to be the light of my life.

I needed a puppy's uncomplicated and pure love. Needed to take care of him and make a home for us both.

I barely knew who I was after the wreck of my nineteen-year marriage. Guillermo and I had only tolerated each other for years, but we probably would have stayed together and just lived miserably if it hadn't been for Estella. For the longest time I told myself I was just imagining things, that Estella was just coming by the *panadería* almost every morning because she liked our coffee and *pan dulce*. Told myself she just wanted to be friends. We'd meet for tacos. We'd go out for drinks. We'd catch a movie together. Guillermo was glad I'd made a friend, said it gave him a chance to go hang out with his buddies without my always checking on him. Estella was fun and we had so much in common. I told myself we were just good friends. Until I found myself with my tongue down her throat and her fingers inside me.

Then I got careless or maybe I wanted Guillermo to know. It'd been going on for several months before he came home unexpectedly, and there we were in the living room, my head between her legs.

He wasn't even angry. We didn't even argue. He just packed his stuff and left. We met with his attorney. I got the house, and he took everything in our accounts. Estella didn't last very long. I didn't have a lot of time for her. Within the year, my mom got really sick, and I took care of her until she died. My dad only lasted a few weeks after her funeral. The doctor said natural causes, no issues, he just passed away in his sleep. I wondered what that would be like, to be loved so much your husband couldn't live without you. They left the *panadería* to me. My brother got their house and the couple of acres it came with.

Little Luz was there for all my grief, for all my loneliness, for all the time afterwards. He was there as I dated woman after woman and they kept breaking my heart. I don't think I ever knew what I was looking for. I just know I never found it.

Luz would come with me to the bakery. He became the unofficial mascot. He wasn't allowed into the kitchen, of course, but he had free run of the little area where we had a couple booths where people sat and ate. Business was good and over the years, I started expanding. I changed the name of the *panadería* from Reyna's Panadería to Mi Luz Panadería. The new sign and all our boxes and bags bore the new logo: a half sun with little Luz's face.

We made all the traditional *pan dulce* the way my parents had taught me: *molletes*—called *conchas* everywhere else—*hornitos*, pink cake, *donas*—Mexican donuts were not American donuts—*marranitos*, *pan de polvo* with cinnamon and sugar, *pan de polvo* with powdered sugar, strawberry jelly rolls, *mantecados*, *churros de cajeta*, *orejas*, tri-colored cookies, *empanadas de camote* and *calabaza* and *piña* and *manzana*, all in all enough *pan dulce* to fill the six-foot cases. I decided to add tacos to the menu, and added *caldo* and *menudo* on weekend mornings. I poured every cent of profit back into the *panadería*. I knocked down one wall and expanded the kitchen and the seating area. More of the college kids started coming around along with families and the old, retired men that needed somewhere to meet up for a few hours every day. I bought an espresso machine the same day I put in wifi. We went from closing at 3 p.m. to 5 p.m. to 7 p.m. to 9 p.m.

I met Elisa when she came in to order *pan dulce* for a reception she was hosting for a friend. I'd never known an artist before and never one that wanted 200 mini *marranitos* and 200 mini *molletes* and 500 heart-shaped *pan de polvo* cookies. While we were talking, she ended up trying some of our *caldo de pollo* with shredded chicken and *calabacitas* and potato and rice and carrots and tomatoes and cilantro and lime juice. Before I knew it, she'd ordered enough *caldo* for a hundred people.

When I was directing the delivery and set up at the reception, Elisa brought me a glass of wine. I mentioned that it had been the favorite wine of an ex. She tilted her head at me for a second and said her ex had taught her to love it. "Nereida," we both said same at the same time. I laughed and said it made us like in-laws of in-laws, that it was too bad there was no word for the ex of an ex. In a low and dramatic voice she said, "The ex of my ex is my friend," and then clasped both my hands with hers.

Elisa was the one I called when the veterinarian told me it'd be best to let Luz go. "The cancer was just too advanced," he said, "and the pain was too much for his little body."

Luz was with me for longer than my marriage. Twenty years of his big eyes and his furry little face. Twenty years of cuddles and walks. I took him almost everywhere with me. During the hot months, I carried him, only allowing his little paws to touch grass and earth. I would think sometimes about that little rhyme, "*ni madre ni padre ni perro que me ladre*," but it was never true for me. Because even though I was otherwise alone in the world—no mother, no father, no husband, no children, sometimes no girlfriend—I always had little Luz.

Until now. So I brought his favorite little sun-and-moon-shaped bacon treats. His favorite toy, Mr. Bebop, the little pig that squeaked when he'd carry him in his jaws, and Shushu, the rainbow glowworm he wouldn't sleep without. I had a thousand different photos of Luz. It took hours to choose my favorites. The base of the altar was his last dog bed and his favorite pillow. I made paper flowers to string everywhere. The last thing I added to the altar was his leash and his collar with the metal tag with his name.

My little Luz.

Feliciana

I don't think this is the right house. I don't know any of these people. I was passing by on the other side of street and saw a young woman I thought was my granddaughter. Her hair is just like hers. Black-black and falling straight past her hips. She was carrying yards and yards of fabric in her arms. All colors, *bien vivos*. Lots of yellow and orange and turquoise and green. And then a bag from the *mercado*, all full of ribbons and lace and spools of thread.

Before the arthritis in my hands got too bad, I used to spend my days making blankets. I'd sell them at the Bargain Bazaar. I made a lot of baby blankets. Those were very popular, because they didn't cost as much as the queen or king size ones. When people would complain my blankets cost too much, I'd tell them, "If you want a cheap blanket, go to Walmart. You won't find any blankets like these there. This is good fabric, everything sewn by hand, even the ruffle edging. I bought the softest, thickest cotton batting and, feel here, I layered it and stitched it into place. This blanket will last you the rest of your life, you'll be able to pass it on to your children!"

No, this girl's not my granddaughter. She looks so serious! My *nieta* was always laughing. But I hear music and voices. *Bien alegres*. And there are people singing. I want to go listen. They won't notice me. I won't make too much noise. I'll just find somewhere to sit. And someone's making tacos—I can smell corn tortillas on the *comal*! Some *bistec* with *cebollitas asadas* and a squeeze of lime would be so delicious!

Yes, there's a little comfy chair in this corner, under the tree, where the breeze is just right. And a young man, so polite, very gentlemanly, just brought me a glass of *agua de jamaica* with a little bit of ice, just like I like it. He says he'll bring me the next plate of tacos.

Qué bonito. There's a lot of people here. I don't know any of them. There are kids playing and running around with a little dog. There are so many flowers. I've never seen so many marigolds at the same time in my life! Then there are people gathered around the woman making tacos, waiting their turn and singing. And all these tables with photos and food and flowers and candles.

I don't think any of those are for me, but no one's telling me I don't belong. *Aquí me quedo*.

This house must belong to that woman right there. Every person that comes in hugs her first. And she keeps pointing in one direction and then another. She's wearing a man's shirt that's too big on her and the bottom of her pants are ragged—she cut them but never hemmed them. I could take care of both those things in just a few minutes. That's how I brought in money when my children were little. Alterations. I'd fix everything: men's suits, missing buttons, sleeve lengths, pants, church dresses, wedding gowns, *quinceañera* dresses, uniforms. So many uniforms: maids, cooks, nurses, mailmen, school uniforms, everything!

How nice! The young man didn't forget me. He brought me a plate with two tacos *de bistec* with cilantro and grilled onion and radish slices and lime wedges. Even two rolled up napkins.

I can't stop looking at the Lady. She's so beautiful. Her face peaceful, round but with strong cheekbones. Intelligent eyes. The clay of her is dark, dark. And now that the sun is setting, all the marigolds in her arms and bursting from her body make it look like she's on fire.

She reminds me of Chela. Chela had eyes like that. Like she was always thinking. When I'd ask her what she was thinking, she'd always make me either laugh or cry. I miss her so much. Our husbands were best friends all their lives. My mother died when I was young. My sisters were all much older than me. I'd never had a best friend until I met Chela. Roberto introduced me to her and Eligio the first time we went to the Saturday night dance at the church hall. I was seventeen. Chela was eighteen. She and Eligio had already been married for two years and had a baby boy.

I loved her so much. We took care of each other's children. We cooked for each other's families. We spent many holidays and birthdays together. At first, we only hugged, sometimes we sat and held each other's hands. It wasn't until after all our children had grown and moved away that she pulled me toward her and kissed me. And I kissed her back. It was nothing like kissing Roberto. I loved my husband, but when Chela touched me, it was like finally, everything was right and nothing was missing. We stayed with our husbands until they died but spent as much time together as we could.

Roberto died first, a heart attack when he was sixty-six. Then Eligio when he was seventy-four. Cancer. Chela and I moved in together. None of our children thought it was odd. It only made sense for two *viejitas* who were best friends to share a house. I never thought I would be the happiest I ever was in my life in my sixties. Every night, Chela slept in my arms. Every morning, her voice was the first sound I heard. And what a thrill I felt, every time I ran my hand down along her naked hip. After so many decades of longing, neither of us cared that our hair had gone grey, our flesh rounded and our skin loose, our joints sometimes stiff. What mattered was that we were free to reach for each other.

Now I'm just waiting for her. She comes from long-lived people. She must be in her nineties already.

I've been looking for her all day. She's not in the house we lived in. She's not in any of her children's houses. I'm not sure if it's been ten years or twenty already since I died. I was starting to forget things while I was still alive. But not Chela. Never Chela. I'm going to finish these delicious *taquitos*. Then I'll get my things and keep on looking. *Ay,* I must be taking too long. I can hear her voice calling my name now.

My heart was always a lit flame for her, my love spilling out of me like all the marigolds spilling out of the Lady's arms.

Maribel

I still can't get used to calling her Elisa. I keep calling her Profe. She says that's not right. I tell her, you teach a class at the university, we get to call you Profe. It just seems disrespectful to call her *Elisa* or *Mssss!*

I don't feel like I know what I'm doing here. No matter what I do, it's just not right. And it's not enough. Profe says my hope has to be bigger than my despair. That I need to transform all this rage into love. But I don't know how to do either of those things.

Most of the time art feels totally useless. Here I am, making this huge altar dedicated to lives lost crossing the border, to all the children lost at residential schools, to murdered and missing Indigenous women, to the Ayotzinapa 43, to the Latin American environmental activists that have been killed. And there's news clippings and names and photos and all my ofrendas and I've laid it all out like I'd sketched it out for Profe to take a look at.

But now that it's all here, it feels like it's nothing. It's just here, in Profe's backyard for as long as this party lasts. Tomorrow, we'll be taking it all down. Sure, she says that we'll document it while it's up and it can be shared online. I'll have all the materials to do an installation anywhere in the future. And she says she's going to introduce me to José Camargo—her friend, she says, her friend—like he's not super famous. We studied his work in one of my classes. My professor literally cried when he told us about the first time he saw José Camargo's work in person.

My altar doesn't *feel* like anything. It just looks like pieces, like a kid's collage. It doesn't come together. It's not one thing. It doesn't build, it doesn't feel natural or inevitable or forceful or anything. It doesn't *coalesce*, like Profe says. It doesn't have any *moments*.

She told me about an installation she saw when she was in college. Amalia Mesa Bains' *Vanidades*. How it had moments where everything paused for her. How she felt alone and immersed, even though she was in a gallery with other people. How much she wanted to touch the hairbrush on the vanity. How in that space she might as well have been smelling her mother's talcum powder and body soap. How the world shifted when she looked at her own face in the mirror and saw César Chávez' face superimposed over hers.

I've only ever made one thing that I felt really worked. It was the project I submitted at the end of my semester with Profe. Mixed media. Part earth, part fabric, partly painted, partly embroidered. A tribute to my parents. They were both musicians, gunned down by drug dealers in some no-name bar in a small town. I was sent to live with my Aunt Rosie in Utah. I was only four. She and my Uncle Bob changed my name from Maribel to Danielle and never spoke to me in Spanish.

They couldn't understand why I'd choose to apply to a university in South Texas. Why I'd go back to where my parents had come from. I applied and got a full scholarship. During my freshman year I drove the couple of miles from the university to the courthouse and changed my name back to Maribel. I let the blonde highlights and the coloring Aunt Rosie had insisted on grow out. I walked in the sun as much as I wanted to and watched my skin darken. I took three years of Spanish and listened to Tejano on the radio and watched *telenovelas* on the Mexican tv channels until I could understand what people were saying.

I'd only ever seen my grandparents once a year when I lived in Utah. I started to spend time with them and my aunts and uncles and cousins. I started to visit my parents in the cemetery. It was in the cemetery that I knew what I wanted to do for my final project for Profe. I sat there on the ground, a bit dazed, as image after image bloomed in my mind. And then I raced home to begin. I'd never worked so hard on anything before. Never spent just hours and hours sitting with it and tracing parts of it with my fingertips and dreaming about it and talking to it. And it would tell me what else was missing. And then there was a morning when I looked at it and it was just *alive*. And I knew I was done.

Pati

Ay, *mira*, it's been twenty-nine years, and she still builds an altar for me. That same photo in a silver frame. *Qué bonito*. And my favorite peonies, without stems, on the lace tablecloth. The first time I held a peony in my hands, I told Emma Elisa they reminded me of the plump bodies of doves. Soft, round, feathered. And look, a plateful of tamales. Chicken with *salsa verde*, each tamal tied with a little strip of corn husk. Like an extra blessing. Like little gifts. They're even still steaming. And a little shot glass with tequila. And a cup of my favorite coffee, that fancy coffee she would special-order for me that tasted like coconut.

I see the Big Flower Lady in the middle of the backyard. There's nowhere you can be that she can't see you. I like the *cempasúchil* but mostly I just see *chichis* and *nalgas* and flowers coming out of her whatchucallit—Emma Elisa says yooohhhnis. I used to ask her all the time why she made so many naked lady statues with breasts and yooohhhnis, and she would say, "*Amá,* it's about a woman's eye seeing a woman. It's about the desires of women. *Los deseos de las mujeres.*" And I would say, "Okay, but make me something else. I don't need woman parts on necklaces or earrings or keychains, *m'ija*. How about flowers? Or the sun and the moon?"

My poor Emma Elisa, all alone. Some years she has someone, but most years, she's alone. I wish I'd been able to give her some sisters and brothers. But she was my only. I didn't tell the doctors they could cut me, but they did. I was only nineteen. Went to the hospital alone. No insurance. The doctors said I was signing for painkillers. My mother said it was probably for the best, because I fell in love and I fell in love and I fell in love and none of them ever stayed. She said those lying doctors were a blessing in disguise, or I would have had twenty kids with twenty different fathers. She'd already raised me and my sisters. She said she didn't want to raise her grandchildren too. She never understood that I just wanted somewhere to belong. I wanted someone to hold me and make me real. I wanted to make a home, a warm pretty place that didn't smell like bleach and fried potatoes. I wanted a man to put his arms around my shoulders, to put his hand on my hip, to keep me warm and weigh me down and fill me and exhaust me. I wanted a home filled with laughter and kisses and affectionate touches. The men came and went, came and went, but mostly it was just me and Emma Elisa.

So I filled our home with flowers and leafy things. Bought us a color tv and soft furniture that I never covered in plastic.

Emma Elisa liked to draw and make things, so I bought her a few things every week: crayons, watercolors, construction paper, Play-Doh … I worked part-time as a cashier at a grocery store and picked up shifts at the Mexican restaurant a few blocks away. I tried not to leave Emma Elisa with my mother too often. She always came back too quiet and sometimes with tear tracks on her face. My best friend Mari had four kids and was a housewife, so mostly Emma Elisa ended up over there. When she got older, she helped care for the little ones, drawing them pictures and keeping them out of trouble. She was always independent. By the time she was twelve, she'd cook herself dinner and do her homework without my having to tell her anything.

When she was sixteen she told me she liked girls, not boys. I'd just woken up and was still wiping the sleep out of my eyes. She said it low, a little nervous, with a look in her eyes like she thought I might hit her or like she might cry. I'd never struck her or even spanked her because I never wanted to be like my mother. I pulled the blanket back and held my arms out to her. She made a little cry, and I held her the way I'd held her when she was a little girl and afraid to sleep when there was thunder. I kissed her temple. "It's okay, *m'ija*, it's okay. You can love whoever you want to love." And she cried, just a few tears, because my Emma Elisa was always strong like that. It took me a few minutes though before I thought to tell her that it would probably be best not to say anything to her grandmother.

I was dating Rubén then. I thought he was going to be the one. He stuck around for a while, but then he left too. And then there was Frankie. And Joel. Emma Elisa went to the community college for a couple years and then moved to Austin to go to UT. David used to take me up there to go see her every other month. He'd take us out to a nice dinner and to go see some of his buddies playing live music here and there. Before Emma Elisa graduated, she introduced me to her girlfriend Luisa and said she was following her back to San Francisco. By then, David was gone and I was seeing Michael. We flew out once to see Emma Elisa in California, and once she took the Greyhound to come spend a few weeks with me here.

And then I met Elías, and he really was the one. He got down on his knee to propose, and I wore his ring. We set a date and picked a cake and sent out invitations and even Mamá liked him. But then that day came. We were going out for lunch, to that little *taquería* we both liked so much on North 10th street with the *tacos de trompo* and the baked potatoes and the good lemonade. He was kissing my hand and I was looking at him and neither of us saw the truck that ran the red light.

We never got to promise each other 'til death do us part. But it was okay, because we'd already promised each other *forever, forever* and that's what it's been. Two years together in life, twenty-nine together in the afterlife. He's visiting his brother's family right now, but he'll be here before long. And he'll take my hand and bring it up to his lips to kiss it and he'll say my name and smile.

Emma Elisa

I don't know what made me start, but once I started I knew I would never stop. It started with small drawings, with crayons and clay and watercolors. I never knew we were poor because there was always food and there was always paper and crayons and paints and clay. Mamá never said anything if I used all the aluminum foil or if I cut up our towels or if I painted on the walls. Almost every day when she came to pick me up after work, she'd bring me something. Not dolls or dresses but construction paper and glue and pipe cleaners and glitter.

As I got older, she bought me pencil sets and charcoals, canvases and acrylics, pastels and self-hardening clay. There was a year I picked up cross stitch and needle point and knitting. I had plastic bins stacked five feet tall with all my supplies and all my projects. Mamá never fussed when I brought in twigs, leaves, wildflower bouquets, clumps of earth, rocks, mesquite bean pods or bits of fallen nests.

This is sort of what my house looks like now that I've lived in it alone since La Lagartija left. What was a three-bedroom house no longer even has a dedicated guest room. There's my bedroom that is also partly a studio, the second bedroom that has always been my studio and the used-to-be guest room that has a bed hidden somewhere under my current projects. The kitchen is mostly clear, except for the breakfast nook, which now has my easel and several canvases. The living room has several towers of books I'm planning to start reading, but there's enough room for at least eight people to sit. And the dining room's free now too. I think I threw everything I had on the dining table and the chairs in the pantry. I'll bring it all back out after the party.

I told everybody they can party and drink all they want, but there's nowhere to sleep except on the floor or in the backyard, where they're free to lay out a blanket or a *sarape* or a sleeping bag. I left out a small pile on the patio along with some old throw pillows in case anyone gets tired.

I want to do this the way Mamá used to tell me she remembered it. Spend all day preparing and laying out the *altares*, stay up all night holding vigil, break bread all together in the morning.

Of course, my friends started drinking the moment they got here. Dusk is falling now. Most of the *altares* are done. Just a few people are still scrambling now with finishing touches. So glad Nora came. She's been making the most amazing tacos all day. I wasn't sure if she was going to be all right. We've been friends for a decade, even dated for a little while, but I'd never known she had a son until she found out he'd died. I kept my distance while she worked on her son's altar. There was a moment there where it seemed like she was flinging marigold petals at it. I could almost see the flowers bleeding in her hands as she twisted the petals off.

José's been a sweetheart with the drinks. I'm so glad he's here too. His first Día de los Muertos without Ismael. I caught him singing earlier while he was handing out drinks. It'd been a while since I'd heard him singing. The world's not right if he's not singing or humming under his breath. He thinks I haven't noticed he's been stuffing his face with my marigolds. If he'd asked, I would have told him to eat as many as he wanted. I'm not saving them for anything. I grew them for today.

I'm glad Antonio's here. He says his wife will come by tonight after she gets out of the hospital. He hasn't said anything, but I think he's a little nervous about how his wife will react to the altar he created. It's so beautiful, it has a marvelous stillness and reverence and simplicity. Photos of his mother, his brother, his first love and the child that was never born. White roses and sunflowers and red roses and pink and red hibiscuses. And all those gorgeous origami birds. I met Antonio at one of my favorite *taquerías*. I usually go at least twice a week after the lunch rush, but I went there early one day since I'd skipped breakfast. The place wasn't busy, and we must have been at least ten feet away from each other. I was busy sketching some new ideas and must have forgotten where I was, since I started singing along with the music playing on the jukebox. It was one of my favorite old songs from an LP my mother had inherited from her father.

I didn't realize I was singing along until Antonio decided to join in too. I looked up in surprise. "I love Los Cadetes de Linares too," he said with the widest smile. Just like that, we were friends. Before long, he told me his story. And I told him there was nothing better than art to pour your life and your stories and your pain and your love into. So he's been trying out new things, reading me poems and stories, showing me sketches, researching different artists I tell him about. This is the first time he's come over to my house. His eyes looked so large as I gave him an impromptu tour through all my messy art rooms.

Maribel came with us too. She kept apologizing every time she reached out to touch some half-formed thing. I laughed and told her none of it would break, and if it did break, there wasn't anything I couldn't fix. I didn't know when I took on the task of teaching a class at the university that I was going to end up loving all of my students. Maribel, though, I can feel it, I'm going to know her for the rest of my life. You can practically feel the insatiable drive to learn, to create, to make sense of it all radiating off her. She's hard on herself, but it makes her exacting and the kind of stubborn you must be to make art.

A couple of years before I turned fifty, everything changed for me. Decades of different cities, with different partners and helping to raise their children for a few years here and there, while working one IT job with health insurance after another. Mind-numbing forty-hour workweeks interrupted by a show on the East Coast, in London, in Paris, and then back to the eight to five. Impossible to describe what it took to split myself between the work that paid the bills and my real work for so many decades. As the years passed, my hands learned to follow what my imagination dreamed, learned to translate what my heart felt into something I could touch.

And then I heard something on the wind. With a sudden ferocity, I wanted to come back to the Valley, to the border, to the Gulf, to the place where I grew up. I wanted the food I grew up with and the music I grew up with. I wanted to live on a palm tree-lined street and for my bougainvillea to climb my mesquite trees and spill color everywhere. I wanted a little home like this one and a life like this one and friends like these. This is where I want to live all the years I have left. In my messy house full of half-finished art. Dreaming things and making things.

Like my Lady Cempasúchil. Her face implacable and joyful. The curve of a generous hip and then a muscled thigh, a rounded shoulder and then a strong forearm. Absence and presence. All these hollow spaces within her to fill with earth, to fill with seed, to offer up to the sunlight. She's been complete for a week now. What I dreamed and what blossomed all coming together. Aflame.

It looks like Sol is finished with her altar for little Luz. She's holding one of his toys in her hands, an unbearable sadness on her face. I'm going to go see if I can get Carlos to play some Ángeles Azules. Sol's never been able to resist a *cumbia*. I'll see if I can pull her away to dance with me, bare feet on the grass, just so I can see her eyes light up again.

The Lady

She made me with her hands. Her hands both cool and molten. She dreamed me, she molded me, she smoothed, shaped and named me. She whispered me, she sang me, she screamed, muttered, growled me. She called, invited, invoked me.

So I came. And I calmed the winds. And I calmed the border blood. I came here, to her home, modest material and human but concentrated with power as if lightning slept in it.

I have been cradling this earth and murmuring to these little blossoms. They are mine and I am theirs. On this night of ancestors, I will keep the peace. For the voices that weep for the spirits flickering through. Enter. You are welcome. But you cannot stay. Lightning lives here.

I will come and go. Blossom and burn. Sing and bloom. Bloom and bloom.

Live and live and live until the day comes when this body will fall to the ground with a thud and lay there, collapsed like a pile of rocks.

breath

Not every god is born knowing they're a god.

I have no memory of being born. No memory of where I was before.

Feathers. Scales. Shells. Red and black.

I wasn't. And then I was. As I am. Never a child. In this body the humans call *man*. Broad shouldered, narrow hipped, sometimes as solid as flesh but mostly made of wind.

I had no language when I was all wind. Language came with this body. Memory came with this body. I knew no emotions before I was flesh.

The priests and philosophers debate which gods are more powerful and what the limits of those powers are. They can't begin to define mine because the wind has no limits.

What they can't understand is that my power is not commanding the wind. My power is born of struggle. I create myself out of the wind again and again. I will myself into flesh. I wrest myself from the wind. Dissolve myself. Create myself. Dissolve myself again. That's what gives me my power. Power over myself is the power of the wind.

And the wind is infinite.

Five centuries after the foreigners destroyed my temples and tried to erase my name, I saw something new. Immense and four petaled. White beasts spreading across the land. Silent and ever in motion. I laughed in delight to see them spinning and spinning. New altars built in my image. New altars that shape my name in the air. These altars they made to convert wind into lightning.

What is the essence of my godhood but wind transformed into lightning?

I loved a human once. I don't know that I'd ever loved anything before her.

She was one of my Voices, listening at all hours to the wind and giving my words to the people. She was more bird than woman, more flame than earth, thunderstorms in her eyes.

I heard her cries of delight as the wind whipped her hair and clothing into a frenzy, saw her feet dancing on the earth as if she could take flight. She wasn't startled when she opened her eyes and saw me fleshing myself into being. I mirrored her movements, swaying as she swayed, my feet as light as hers moving across the earth.

I didn't touch her. Not even when the wind gentled. Not even when the clouds traveled to the east, revealing the light of the setting sun in the west.

She only watched me as I came closer. Close enough to feel the push of air as she caught her breath in our sudden stillness. We were so close I could see nothing but her golden eyes.

The humans have spent centuries measuring themselves, wanting to know how they were made. How much water, how much earth, how much fire. They try to calculate the weight of a soul. Tell stories about lightning creating life. Find ways to push death a little further out.

They never ask how much wind they are composed of—though they understand the end of breath is the end of life.

I gave them all breath.

And by giving them breath, I gave them language. I gave them song. I gave them sighs and whispers, murmurs, moans and cries.

I didn't want the humans to rut mindlessly in the fields. To know nothing but heat and the slaking of appetite. I wanted them to know what I know. To feel what I feel. To touch the way I touch. Life isn't life without desire. I wanted them to have the capacity to worship each other the way I worshipped her. I became flesh so that I could touch her. Her touch converted my flesh into lightning.

I gave them breath so they could exist in flesh, and I gave them breath so they could transcend that flesh.

Given how short human lives are, you'd think that after five centuries, the Voices wouldn't know how to listen anymore. But I heard one of them, exclaiming in wonder and falling to their knees at the foot of my new altars. Their soul rendered absolute delight. "Borders of blood," they cried, "the god is healing the borders of blood!"

So much joy in all their Voices. I leaned in close to hear their thoughts. Felt how the histories had weighed upon them. How they could hear the blood-soaked earth whimper and scream in its pain. Day after day and year after year and century after century, so much blood in the earth. Until it came to pass that a mist of blood had risen up from the ground. A blood mist fed by the never-ending spilling of blood. My Voices could see that mist. Could feel it on their skin. Feel it invading their lungs. Feel it poisoning their flesh.

And then they saw the great wings slowly swimming through the air, cleansing it, transforming it, singing it pure again. And the Voices rejoiced and I heard their songs of praise and gratitude.

My heart was gladdened to hear they understood. As the immense white beasts had brought me great joy, I had decided they could do more than convert wind to lightning. The humans who think only pain and tears cleanse have it wrong. Pleasure and song are also medicine. And what is the wind if not ecstasy, sometimes gentle, sometimes fierce, always wild?

It begins with a breath. Breath on skin.

The awestruck wonder of being allowed so close.

It was an eternity before she allowed me to touch.

I danced with her when the storms approached, when the storms raged, when the storms quieted. I held out my hand to her, but she never took it. When I'd take a step toward her, she'd step away. I brought her sweet fruits and traced with my eyes the path the juice took that dripped from her lips, that dripped on her hands, that made her laugh. I sang her songs until she curled up on the grass, until she closed her eyes and tears escaped from them, until one evening she fell asleep while listening, cradled by my voice. I kept vigil over her sleep.

I did not touch. She had not given her permission.

I did look. Marveled at her dark lashes, the dreaming movements of her eyes. Watched her fingers comb lightly through the green blades of grass, as if she was caressing a lover's chest. I watched her side rise and fall with her breath. Her limbs so still. I laid myself beside her. Far away enough that even if I'd stretched out my arm straight all the way in front of me, I wouldn't have been able to touch her.

And I was watching her when she opened her eyes. She saw me and arched her brow.

What poor creatures these humans must be who do not believe in the gods of the wind. What a poor world it would be without the wind, without the waves, without trees. Trees would not be trees without the wind. The wind makes them strong. Makes them live. My Voices say the sound of the wind through the trees is the sound of my desire. The groaning of heavy limbs, the creaking of twigs, the slapping whispering shushing of leaves, the nearly silent song of trees in the moonlight.

I am a god of desire.

One desire is all desires. The desire to exist. The desire to create. The desire to grow. The desire to change. The desire to run. To be free. To become. To love. To sate appetite. To feel pleasure. To give pleasure. To touch the divine. How do you know god without desire?

Worship me like this. With hunger. Without measuring the costs. With clenched teeth and trembling thighs and shuddering breaths. Worship me beyond reason.

And we will remake the world with wind.

I became flesh on the shore as the sun was setting. She was dancing with the waves, collecting shells, singing low and sweet. A song I had sung to her more than once. She laughed when she saw me and held out what she'd been holding in her hand. I took it carefully. Heard it whispering. I traced the flared lip of the conch with my thumb, thought of how its pink interior echoed the color of the sky. And as I turned it one way and another, I realized that she had carved into the conch so that even a slight movement changed the sound the wind made moving through it. Sweet. Rough. High. Low. Loud. Soft. At certain angles to the wind, it seemed I could hear it singing with three distinct voices.

She laughed to see the wonderment on my face. Came close enough for me to see the cord she was now holding. She pushed one end through one of the holes she had bored into the conch and then knotted both ends. She held it up with both hands, and I knelt so she could hang it from my neck.

She didn't move away. I looked up. She rested her hands on my shoulders and looked into my eyes.

I didn't move. I didn't breathe.

She stepped closer, cupped the back of my neck in her hands. Stood so close that a deep breath would make my lips graze the skin over her ribs. Her eyes wide, her jaw set, her mouth serious. She breathed and I breathed and my lips felt the sun- and sea-soaked warmth of her.

How do you worship a god who will not worship you in return?

I was neither sleeping nor silent nor subdued for five hundred years. But time doesn't pass the same for gods as it does for mortals. I spent decades that felt like minutes in the wind, running over the face of the world. I dove in and out of the ocean, skimmed mountaintops, twisted and glided across the night skies. I did the things gods do. It's only that there isn't much to do when the world isn't being created or saved or changed. Once things are set into motion, there isn't all that much to do. My Voices still called out to me, but there weren't as many of them as before. And they asked for very little.

There was nothing for me to ask of them.

In the centuries after she was gone, it hurt to be flesh. To become flesh and know there was no hope of feeling her touch. When I was the wind, I could say she was everywhere. That some trace of her skimmed the skies and the trees with me. That I could hear her laughter when I soared over the ocean waves.

It struck me with terror, the thought of living in my memories of her. That playing and replaying my thousand memories of her would make them lose their crispness. That I'd begin to change the details. That I'd forget the sound of her voice, the scent of her skin, the way she always looked at me, as if she could see the wind my flesh was made of. What if I forgot the way she'd scowl when she was angry, how she'd growl when she'd bite my thighs, how she couldn't sleep if she was hungry? What if I forgot her favorite song or how she'd sing it?

What if I willed myself to forget one day when the loss was too much?

Anyone not irrevocably changed by loss has not suffered a true loss.

It is no easy thing to cleanse the land. Nature is always working the earth. But humans are talented when it comes to shitting on things, to corroding and polluting them, to destroying the balance in ways that tempt Nature to upend everything. We gods do our best to save the world and the humans living on it. Most of them don't deserve chaos and earthquakes, fire and pain and agonizing deaths. Sometimes, though, it is tempting to let Nature lose its patience and rip away the humans. To let the fungi and the flora work and rework the earth, to let the earth in its slow revolutions cleanse itself of chemicals and radiation, to let the green things reclaim asphalt and cities, to let the animals move as Nature dictates, reshaping the earth until it is bountiful again.

It is no easy thing to clear the blood mist. I know the wind. I know desire. I know sound. But cleansing anything requires a reshaping of time. I will myself to have hands more immense than any I have had before. With those immense hands, I twist the wind until I can pull and shape time.

Time cannot be reversed. But like the wind, it can be willed into different shapes, different movements, different paths. The wind is a delight in my hands, but not time. Time is molten hot. Time is an agony to manipulate. My flesh blackens and melts away, but I keep at it. I will myself back into flesh, again and again. And there is that single Voice, screaming and singing praises and prayers.

After all, what is physical pain, when I will never stop grieving her loss? She would have loved the spinning white beasts. She would have danced with them. She would have decided to live where she could always see them, day and night. She would have called them by my name.

The last time I kissed her hand was like the first time. The last time before her eyes closed and her flesh began to cool. The first time, that day by the ocean, me kneeling before her, one of her hands cupped my cheek. I pressed my lips to her hand. From her hand to the bare skin at her midriff. Oh, the beauty of quivering flesh. Hers. Mine. The want to touch and, finally, finally to be allowed close enough. To make worship of this too.

She sank to her knees, fed herself with my mouth. We left no part of each other untouched. This was what was holy of the body. Separate and never separate. She lived her entire life for me. I lived my entire life in the time I had with her. I learned every line as it formed, slowed my days so that I could watch the grey as it conquered the black of her hair. I loved her limbs more, not less, as her steps began to falter. Loved her eyes more, not less, as they clouded over. My beautiful one, made of wind even more than I was. Master that she was, even in her solid flesh, of transcendence and speed, of delight and worship.

My beautiful one, all of this is for you.

prophecy

inspired in part by the painting by Octavio Quintanilla, hoy pensé en ti

It wasn't the last time.

They thought if they were ruthless enough, that it would be the last time. While they were alive, they were a threat. So they said, watch them. So they said, kill them. So they said, desecrate the bodies. So they said, let their blood soak the earth. Infect them with fear so they will never resist again. Silence them so that they will disappear. And the years will pass, and everyone will forget. No memory, no threat.

But time isn't a straight line. Time is a spiral. Everything comes around again. Nothing ever dies. Not forever.

The songs rose up from the earth. The songs surged from the fire. The songs arrived on the wind. They flowed down the river and washed up on the shore. Songs may be sung by the living, but both the living and the dead can hear them. And in the places where the line between the living and the dead is thin, the songs made the line grow thinner.

Prophecies are a spiral. Eagles and condors. Dancers and dreamers. The living and the dead. North and South. Sun rising and sun setting. It wasn't that they began again. The dancers had never stopped dancing. And the dreamers had never stopped dreaming.

Those in the South wore black. Tattooed themselves with calaveras and black flames. In the North, the ghost shirts were brought out of hiding, were reclaimed from museums and collections, were made by young hands. Black crows and buffalos and stars and thunderbirds.

As all the feminine deities had been crushed, buried, obscured, and renamed, so the day came when they were resurrected. So the day came when the old names and the new names were woven together in a long chain of songs. Prayers and offerings. Dance and smoke. Jeweled seed and flower. And the neverending interwoven name was sung by a few voices and then a thousand voices and then a thousand thousand voices.

And for each one that stood there were ten thousand ghosts that stood with them. Ten thousand ghosts, some without names, some without faces, some without bodies, only hearts beating steady. Crimson knots of flame.

And together they took the first step. The living and the dead in interlocking circles, dancing through the days and through the nights. There was no fear of blood spilling because there was no blood to spill.

And what was lost was regained. What was forgotten was remembered. And stories that had not been heard for centuries were told again. And the wounds of the Conquest were cleansed and what had been ripped asunder was joined again. And the earth sighed when the feet moving in a circle dance, sometimes whisper soft, sometimes hard as drums, began to push out pollution and contamination. All the waters of the earth rippled clean, releasing what did not belong.

And there were those who trembled in fear of change. Whose raging hearts could not understand that what had been stolen was not theirs. Those who fired weapons at ghosts and shrieked when the ghosts didn't fall to the ground. Those who could never understand that time was a spiral. And the earth remained impassive, for it delighted in transformation and renewal. And understood that renewal sometimes encompassed destruction.

Song and dance and drumming feet. After the Great Rain, the world was made anew. And the horses ran free. And the buffalo multiplied. The leaves were reborn and the lightning was reborn and the dew was reborn and the songs were sung. Neverending dances. And the wind was the wind.

And nothing was stolen.

And life was only what was given and received in gratitude.